Sean bent his head and touched his lips to her hair. Then to her cheekbone; then, still holding her hands behind her back, he nudged her head upwards and claimed her lips with his own.

'Mmm,' he murmured, drawing them away from hers. 'You ought to be kissed more often.'

'I don't think I——'

'There's such a thing,' Sean responded, dropping a trail of chilli-hot kisses across her forehead and down to her ear, 'as thinking too much.'

'You said you wouldn't make a pass at me.'

'This isn't a pass,' Sean reasonably replied. 'It's only a kiss.'

His tongue, his lips, his hands, were moving with all the tantalising restlessness that was quintessentially Sean: touching and teasing, then drifting on almost before she could absorb each sensation enough to respond to it.

'Just——' he bent down and dropped the lightest of kisses on the end of her nose '——a kiss.'

WE HOPE you're enjoying our new addition to our Contemporary Romance series—stories which take a light-hearted look at the Zodiac and show that love can be written in the stars!

Every month you can get to know a different combination of star-crossed lovers, with one story that follows the fortunes of a hero or heroine when they embark on the romance of a lifetime with somebody born under another sign of the Zodiac. This month features a sizzling love-affair between **Taurus** and **Aquarius**.

To find out more fascinating facts about this month's featured star sign, turn to the back pages of this book. . .

ABOUT THIS MONTH'S AUTHOR

Sally Cook says: 'I'm a Taurean myself, like Emma in A DESIRE TO LOVE, which I wrote for a Newport-based Taurean friend. Taureans seem to stick together: at least half of my close friends fall under the same sign, and to me that's more than a coincidence.

'Astrologers often say Taurus and Aquarius is a bad combination, but I loved an Aquarian man once, and so have many of my Taurus friends. So this is for Philip too—and for all the other Taurus-Aquarius couples out there.'

A DESIRE TO LOVE

BY

SALLY COOK

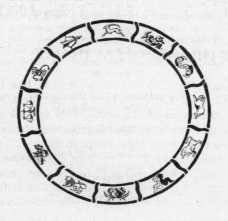

MILLS & BOON LIMITED
ETON HOUSE   18–24 PARADISE ROAD
RICHMOND   SURREY   TW9 1SR

First published in Great Britain 1991
by Mills & Boon Limited

© Sally Cook 1991

Australian copyright 1991
Philippine copyright 1991
This edition 1991

ISBN 0 263 77115 6

STARSIGN ROMANCES is a trademark of Harlequin Enterprises
B.V., Fribourg Branch. Mills and Boon is an authorised user.

Set in 10 on 11½ pt Linotron Plantin
01-9104-56106 Z
Typeset in Great Britain by Centracet, Cambridge
Made and printed in Great Britain

CHAPTER ONE

'COME on, come *on*,' Emma Morgan muttered, as the car in front of her—a battered old blue Peugeot—eased off from the traffic-lights, a good twenty seconds *after* they had turned green. Obviously the driver wasn't heading for the five-thirty ferry, but she was, and unless he got a move on she was going to miss it.

Hugging the Peugeot's tail, her Volvo estate crawled down Western Esplanade, round the West Gate roundabout, past Mayflower Park—and there at last was the Town Quay, with the red funnel of the ferry still mercifully looming up behind the low buildings of the terminal.

To her surprise the Peugeot swung into the terminal forecourt, whence she rapidly followed it, her eyes anxiously scanning the shortening queue of cars. How many had already boarded? Would there be enough room? She shouldn't have left it this late, not without booking her space. She rarely took the long crossing to the Isle of Wight, but it hadn't needed experience, only common sense, to tell her that the five-thirty would be busy.

Which it was. The queue had almost disappeared, but so had the space on the car deck. Stewards on the Isle of Wight ferries always squeezed the cars tight, but even then she wasn't sure. . .

She wound down her car window, ignoring the brisk wind that whipped off Southampton Water, and craned her head out to see what the stewards were up to.

One of them came striding towards her, the papers on his clipboard flapping in the breeze. 'You booked, love?'

Emma's spirits sank. Oh, no. It would be just the end she needed to a lousy day, if her decision to leave the return crossing open backfired on her now.

She scraped up a rather desperate smile. 'Not on this particular sailing, no. I've got my ticket, but I . . . I wasn't sure. . .'

'You always ought to book.'

'Surely you can find a space somewhere? Can't you squeeze me in next to that white van?'

'The bloke in front of you'll have to go there.'

The sadist. The rotten sadist. He actually seemed to be enjoying her predicament!

'Looks like thee or me,' a lively male voice chimed in.

Emma's eyes flickered from the steward to the man who had, without her noticing, come up behind him. He was obviously the Peugeot driver, a guess confirmed when she glanced at his car and saw the driver's door gaping open.

She gave him a decidedly sour look, half because he seemed so unreasonably cheerful, and half because she couldn't help blaming him for making her late. The tortoise of Western Esplanade! It was all right for him, he'd get the space next to the white van.

'That's about it, sir,' the steward agreed.

'I knew you should have overtaken me,' the Peugeot driver said cheerily.

'Well, thank you! It's really helpful to be told that now!'

'Cool it. What I meant was, that would have saved me my crisis of conscience.'

'Your *what*?'

'I mean, just one of you, left on the shore. There's a certain poetic elegance about it, but it won't be much fun, will it, sitting here watching us sail off on the ebb tide without you?'

What on earth was he going on about? Emma hastily backtracked, trying to recall his opening line. Which she couldn't, but it did at least sink in on her that he felt guilty about grabbing the last place.

'Do you mean you might. . .?' she faltered. 'Is there any chance. . .?'

'When's the next ferry?' the tortoise asked, turning to the steward.

'Not till seven-fifteen, sir.'

'As long as that! I thought you had umpteen sailings an hour.'

'Not this time of year: we started the winter timetable last week.'

'Oh.' The tortoise's face fell dramatically. Well, wasn't that nice? Emma thought grouchily. If he'd only had to wait ten minutes he might have let her on instead of him—but then, she wouldn't have minded waiting ten minutes herself. Now he knew it would be an hour and three quarters, though, he would obviously give up on his half-formed idea of being chivalrous.

But he hadn't given up yet, to judge by the way his face lifted in a manner that spelled out 'bright idea'. He moved a step closer. The steward stepped aside, and the tortoise leaned a long hand on the lower frame of Emma's open window and bent down to gaze at her.

He had striking light blue eyes, which held hers in a direct way she found disconcerting. She knew she ought to put on an appealing expression, but she wasn't the type—or in the mood—for flirtatious games, and that levelly appraising look flustered her.

'You're not going to Newport, by any chance?'

'Yes, I am, actually.'

'Fancy giving me a lift?'

'A lift!'

'We compromise.' The tortoise gave her a broad, lazy smile. 'Obviously neither of us wants to be left behind, but my car hasn't any strong feelings either way. So I was thinking, I could come in your car. I'll leave mine here, you give me a lift into Newport, then I'll come back and get it in the morning.'

Emma stared at him. 'That's about the most harebrained scheme I've ever heard. For heaven's sake, you'd have to do the crossing *three times*. All right,' she went on, guiltily aware that he was at least making an effort, 'it's kind of you to suggest it. But you obviously haven't thought it through.'

'I quite like ferry crossings.'

'We've got to finish loading now, sir.'

The tortoise glanced round at the steward. 'Won't be a minute,' he said airily. 'We're just coming to an agreement. Where's the best place for me to park overnight? Over there?'

'I don't know as I can allow you to leave your car behind, sir.'

'Fiddlesticks! If I can be gallant, so can you.'

Without waiting for a response he strode breezily—and unhurriedly—back to his open car, took his time about reversing it out of the narrow space between Emma's front bumper and the ferry gangway, and drove it to the far end of the forecourt.

Emma watched these proceedings open-mouthed. The tortoise emerged from his car, locked it, and strode back towards hers.

He was a tall man, in his thirties, she guessed, and dressed in a manner somewhere between eccentric and scruffy, with a blue and white checked blazer flapping open over a red shirt, and a disreputable-looking pair of blue jeans. A loosely knitted scarf was looped round his neck. His hair was mouse-brown, fine and rather unruly, not to mention an inch too long for smartness. But the body that he moved with such lithe ease looked to be in good condition—broad-shouldered, narrow-hipped, long-legged—and his face bore an appealing stamp of good humour. She'd barely taken in his features at first, only those startling blue eyes and the overall impression of likeability, but they were good, she saw now: a long straight nose, a decided chin, and a well-shaped mouth that looked as if it were made to smile.

In fact he was quite something—as he must know very well, she thought uncomfortably as he approached. Not many men underrated their own attractiveness, and in his bizarre way this man had plenty—plus the kind of solid self-confidence that suggested women generally agreed with his own opinion of himself.

How much, she wondered, had her own brunette good looks to do with his snap decision? And what might he expect in return for his quixotic gesture?

She didn't approve of giving strangers lifts at the best of times, and this was no harmless little old lady. But then, neither did she want to miss the ferry. . .

The tortoise opened her passenger door, folded a pair of very long legs into the car, and announced, 'Sean,' holding out his hand with a smile.

Emma recollected herself sufficiently to put her hand in his and say, 'Emma—Emma Morgan,' in reply.

'Nice to meet you, Emma.' She didn't reply to this, being busily engaged in manoeuvring her estate car into the tiny space that was left on the car deck.

Closer, the steward signalled; and closer. Then he raised his palm towards her, and Emma, sighing in relief, switched off the ignition and began to wind up the window.

'Need anything up on deck?' Sean asked.

She gave him a wary sideways glance. Curse it. It hadn't sunk in before that she had just condemned herself to an hour and a half of his company.

'Just my handbag—and a book to read.'

'Sure you need the book?'

'Actually I'm looking forward to getting back to it.'

She glared at him, daring him to complain, then reached out her hand for the fat Dorothy Dunnett novel she had left on the back seat.

In single file, they made their way up the narrow stairway to the main passenger deck. It was crowded. Emma glanced at the windows, took in an expanse of choppy grey, and decided she would be blown to bits if she went on to the top deck.

'The bar, don't you think?' Sean suggested. 'If you don't mind the smoke. What're you drinking?'

'I ought to get you one really.'

'So you ought,' he cheerfully agreed. 'Mine's a half of something long and wet.'

'Bitter?'

'Or lager, I'm not fussed. Shall we sit over here?'

'Er—fine.'

She dropped her book on the seat next to the one he had taken, then fought her way across to the bar, which was, of course, even busier than everywhere else on the ferry.

She stationed herself at the back of the press of customers, shoved her hands in the pockets of her bottle-green waxed cotton jacket, and gave way to a scowl.

It was a relief, admittedly, that she had scraped on to the ferry, but, the more she considered it, the less she relished the price she would have to pay.

Sean didn't look like a murderer or a rapist—not that she had ever known one—and she wasn't quaking with fear at the thought of the twenty-minute drive from the

Cowes terminal to Newport. She was more worried about the question of how he would get back to Cowes the next morning. He'd need to reach Southampton reasonably early if he wasn't to be lumbered with heavy parking charges by the Red Funnel people, and he obviously hadn't given a thought to how he was going to do the journey. She felt responsible now, and she could well imagine that she'd end up driving him herself.

It even niggled her that she was stuck with buying him a drink. Of course she owed it to him, and she wouldn't have wriggled out of the obligation, but she minded about the cost, quite apart from the annoyance of standing in this jostling crush when she was feeling tired to death. And it would be rude, she supposed, not to drink with him. Admittedly she was thirsty, but if she had been on her own she would have stuck it out till she got home.

The whole thing was crazy, absolutely crazy. He was mad to have suggested leaving his car behind, and she was almost as mad to have agreed. Hadn't she had enough dealings with rackety men to have learned to give them the widest of wide berths?

'Cheer up, love, we haven't sunk yet.'

'Sorry.' Caught up in her gloomy thoughts, she hadn't even realised that the queue had evaporated, and the barman was waiting to serve her. He was right, too, she *was* being a terrible grump. She forced a smile, and gave him her order for a half of lager and an orange juice.

It wasn't the tortoise's fault, after all, that she had had a wretched day. In fact, his well-intentioned—if ludicrous—gesture had been the only reasonably pleasant thing that had happened to her.

An interesting meeting, that was what it was. Now why had those words come into her head? Of course: her horoscope. Her friend Judy had read it out the day

before, from the daily forecasts that she, Judy, had
written for the *Newport Herald*.

After which they had had their familiar altercation,
Emma objecting that Judy always made her forecasts too
cheerful, and Judy protesting that that was perfectly
reasonable of her, since nobody wanted to read gloomy
predictions every day.

'So what you mean is,' Emma had complained, 'you
write the Taurus forecasts just to jolly me along.'

'You and my mum. And the Sagittarius for Tom, and
the Scorpio for Fred Mullins, and the Pisces for me.'

'Disgraceful!'

'Not really,' Judy had defended herself. 'All good
writers bear in mind what their readers want to be told,
and I simply use the readers I know personally as
examples. And I've told you often enough, Em, that the
stars don't determine what will happen to us, they just
influence it in subtle ways. So there's nothing to stop an
astrologer choosing to interpret those influences
positively.'

'What made you say "interesting meetings", then?'

'A conjunction of the Moon and Saturn in Capricorn,
which really does suggest that strange and significant
things are going to happen to lots of Taureans
tomorrow.'

Strange and significant! That was rather an over-the-
top description for getting lumbered with giving a nut-
case a lift, Emma thought ruefully. But then, Judy
always acknowledged that a general daily forecast could
never be a hundred per cent accurate. In fact she had
gone on to review Emma's personal chart, and to warn
her that Mercury was ominously placed, and she
shouldn't expect too much from her expedition—which
had certainly turned out to be an accurate prediction.

In fact the day had left her with worries large enough

that, compared to them, Sean the tortoise hardly rated a second thought.

But when she got back to him with the drinks, it was to find that he had solved one problem already. 'Frank here,' he explained, gesturing to the lorry driver to whom he had been chatting, 'says he's got to take another load out of Newport in the morning. That's a bit of luck, isn't it? He'll be able to drop me back at the terminal. All I've got to do is get to his depot on the Riverside Industrial Estate by—what time did you say, Frank?'

'Six-thirty should do it.'

'I'd better give you a lift there,' Emma offered.

'No need. Newport isn't that big, I'll be able to walk.' He patted the bench next to him. 'Have a pew, and tell me what's up.'

'Nothing, really. I'm sorry if I seem a bit low. It was kind of you to let me on the boat: thank you.'

'Forget it. What are you rushing back for? To make your old man's tea?'

She didn't have an 'old man'—or a young one, come to that—but it didn't seem like a sensible idea to tell Sean so.

'Actually it's my son I'm really worried about. I told him I expected to get the four o'clock ferry home, and he gets very anxious when I'm late.'

'Who's looking after him?'

'A friend. He'll be all right, but I still don't like to let him down.'

'So why are you late?'

She shrugged. 'A bad day.'

'Work or pleasure?'

'Oh, work.'

'Bad days are usually the ones where I throw in the towel early.'

'Maybe you're not stuck with bills to pay.'

'Sorry, that was facetious of me.' His eyes were still fixed on her, their expression mingling curiosity with an easy friendliness. 'What is it you do?'

'I make and sell patchwork quilts.'

She thought that would shut him up; it usually did with men. But instead he reacted with unmistakable interest, saying cheerfully, 'Tell me about it.'

So she did. At first she spoke haltingly, but soon the whole story came gushing out like oil from a newly struck well. He was a good listener, and she hadn't come across too many of those recently. And unlike her friends he didn't clog or crowd her with sympathy she couldn't handle: he just listened.

Ever since college, Emma explained, she had been running her own small business, designing and making quilts, and teaching patchwork and quilting. It had done well, too, in its small way; but she hadn't ever intended to make a proper living out of it, just to. . .

Her story wouldn't make any sense, she realised, unless she told him about Neil. She hadn't meant to do that. Oh, why not? One rackety man hearing about another—it might even serve to warn him off!

She and Neil had married when she was twenty, and still in college. Neil had been a student too back in those days, but he had thrown it up when Emma became accidentally pregnant, and taken a job in a bookmaker's.

At first she had thought it adult and responsible of him: it was only later that she had realised his studies had been foundering, and he had really been choosing— as always—to take an easy way out.

The job hadn't lasted, of course. Neil's jobs never did. All their married life he had moved from job to job, and the moves had rarely been promotions. They would have been strapped for money from the first, if he hadn't inherited some from his grandfather. That had bought

them Seagulls, their lovely house on the south side of the
Island, with its wide windows overlooking the sea, and
long narrow garden tumbling down the cliffs to the
shore.

Seagulls had been home to them and to Duncan, their
son, for nine years. Then Neil had taken a job as a long-
distance lorry driver. It had just seemed like another job
at the time—indeed, it had suited them both better than
most of those he found. For a fortnight the house had
been pleasantly peaceful. Emma had really enjoyed being
alone with Duncan, and taking a break from the rows
that, by then, had destroyed all the joy in their marriage.
Then the policeman had come to the door.

Neil had been dead by the time the policeman told
her. He had been overtaking another lorry while
approaching a bend, on a narrow stretch of road in the
Midlands. When another lorry had appeared, coming
straight towards him, there had been nothing he could
do.

Emma had still been numb at the news when she
discovered the rest: the debts Neil hadn't told her about,
the overdraft he had negotiated alone, the insurance
policy he had allowed to lapse almost a year earlier. She
had always thought they were getting by, but in fact the
crisis had been creeping steadily closer. It was cold
comfort, though, to discover that even had Neil lived
they would have lost Seagulls.

Her life had seemed so secure. It hadn't always been
happy, but she had always felt safe, the days a steady
progression of small troubles and small pleasures. Then
the whole house of cards had come crashing down.

She had done what she could: selling the house and
moving into a much smaller one in Newport, paying the
creditors and negotiating a proper overdraft at the bank.
The bank manager had agreed that her best prospects

lay in building up her existing business, and with dogged determination she had set about doing that.

There were times, though, when determination didn't seem enough. Nobody could question her skill as a quiltmaker, but she had never pretended to be a whizz as a saleswoman. Before Neil's death she had never worried much about sales, being content to let her stock pile up, and rejoicing when the occasional big item sold. Now she not only had to make more quilts, she had to sell many, many more quilts—and, the more desperate she became, the fewer buyers she seemed to find.

Her slim shoulders shook as she described her efforts to Sean. The ghastly mornings when she would fortify herself with black coffee, then work through the phone book ringing shop after shop. The nightmare days spent walking cold into little craft shops, with photos of her designs under her arm and samples waiting in the car outside. The possible customers who turned out to be indifferent or rude—or, worse, to offer admiration for her work and sympathy for her plight, but nothing more tangible.

Endless efforts to sell her work on the Island had made no impression at all on that detestable overdraft, so now she had forced herself to try the mainland. She had spent all day traipsing round craft shops and department stores in Southampton, and everywhere she had drawn a blank.

She had been telling herself she wouldn't go home until she made a sale, but the afternoon had drawn on and on, and not one shop had shown her more than a flicker of interest.

'That's rough,' Sean said gently. 'But let me get this straight. You're sure your work's up to standard, and it's just that you're no good at selling it?'

Emma nodded. 'The quilts are first rate, there's no

doubt about that. I've won a couple of national competitions, and everyone says I've a good eye for colour and design. It's me as a saleswoman who's a dead loss. I don't really know how to go about it, and I hate it so much. I'm sure that comes across. I wish I could get somebody else to do the selling for me, but I've gone through it all with the bank manager, and there's no way I could afford to pay anyone.'

'It'll come in time. You'll get used to it, and if your work's really good then one day you'll make a breakthrough. The thing is not to get upset. If people don't want to buy, that's their loss. You just have to keep your confidence in what you're doing.'

'It's all right for you to say that.' Emma sighed. 'You're obviously the kind of person who'd enjoy selling things, but I'm not.'

'You're right, actually—I was a salesman for a while. Selling good stuff always struck me as a doddle, although once I was stuck selling equipment I thought was useless, and that I couldn't stomach.' He drained his drink, and set the glass back down. 'There are always solutions to any problem if you think for long enough, though. Don't let it get you down. I'm sure the bank manager won't turn you on to the street tomorrow.'

'True, but in the long run I've got to do something, and I just can't think what.'

'Maybe inspiration will strike me.' He grinned at her. Her own misery clearly hadn't dented his good humour, but she couldn't be offended at his cheerfulness, which in a strange way wasn't lacking in sympathy. 'I can't say it does right now, though. What you need is a change of scene. Come out on deck. It's not much of a change, but it's the best I can offer at the moment.'

'Oh, all right.' Emma glanced at her book, but she knew she wasn't in a frame of mind to concentrate on the story. And it wouldn't do to sit here and grow maudlin over her orange juice, so she might as well let the wind whip some backbone into her.

By the time they emerged on to the open deck the crossing—a short one, even if it was the longest of those connecting the Isle of Wight to the mainland—was already more than half over, and the ferry had left Southampton Water for the Solent. Sean made for the front rail. They were close enough to make out the buildings and boats of Cowes harbour, a brilliant white against the steely blue of water and sky.

'Looks good,' he murmured, eyes on the view.

Emma moved forward to join him, pushing an errant hank of chestnut hair out of her face. The approach to Cowes never failed to lift her spirits, though this time they only rose from rock-bottom to just below normal.

Come to that, it had helped her, in an odd way, to unburden herself. Normally she was careful not to whine to her friends, but perhaps she had been keeping her worries too much to herself, she thought suddenly. Later it might embarrass her to think how frank she had been, but at that moment she simply felt the stirrings of a liking for Sean. Maybe he did share all Neil's worst characteristics, but she wasn't married to *him*—and again, like Neil, he had the kind of effortless charm that made him a very enjoyable temporary companion.

'You like boats?' she asked, not knowing what else to say.

'Now why else would I opt to do the longest ferry crossing to the Island three times over?'

'I don't know: it's a mystery to me.'

'You think I'm crazy?' He turned to her and grinned.

She shrugged awkwardly, though it was apparent that he hadn't taken any offence. 'Not crazy,' she amended. 'A bit eccentric, perhaps.'

'True. I guess I don't rate security as high as you do; what I like is unpredictability. I like being able to take off when I choose, I like having strange things happen. Strange things often happen on ferries, which is one reason why I enjoy them so.'

Emma let out a short bark of laughter.

'Now what's so funny?'

'To tell the truth, I'd been feeling guilty for having bored you with my problems, then it suddenly struck me that you hadn't been bored at all.'

'Of course not. I'm not often bored, and never by beautiful women.'

She tensed. He didn't seem to notice it, but his words had taken away all her momentary pleasure in the encounter. In its place she felt, acutely, both a pang of raw loneliness, and a terror that the longing to cure it might beguile her into another disastrous relationship.

All right, she was over-reacting, and she knew it, but mere thought couldn't take the feeling away.

'It's too windy out here for me,' she said in a sharper voice. 'I'm going back down again.'

'Want me to come?'

'No; no, I'll read for a while.'

'OK, see you back at the car.'

He had turned back to watch the harbour approach even before she reached the steps.

So why shouldn't he? Emma reminded herself, her eyes lingering just a fraction too long on the back of his checked blazer. After all, what was she to him but another interesting encounter on a ferry? She'd drop him off in Newport, and then it was a hundred to one she'd never see him again.

Which was all very well in its way—at least she'd never have to face up to regret at having told him too much about her problems—but it wasn't—wasn't *right*, somehow.

She wasn't like him, that was the thing. She didn't like life to be a succession of casual encounters with passing strangers. All her pleasures came from the comfort of a daily routine, friends and relatives she knew well—in fact, it could all be summed up by that leaden word 'security'. People like Neil might scoff—indeed Neil had done, regularly—but she couldn't change her basic temperament. As Judy told her, she was a typical Taurean. Quicksilver encounters, and sympathy no sooner given than forgotten, were no real joy to her. They only brought heartache and, however pointlessly, the longing for more.

Although she certainly didn't want more from the tortoise of Western Esplanade, she firmly reminded herself, retracing her steps to the bar and searching for her place among the fat pages of Dorothy Dunnett's latest.

But she had barely read a paragraph when she was interrupted by a peremptory female voice announcing, 'Emma. Fancy seeing you here.'

'Oh, hello, Mrs Frazer.' She mustered a smile, and forced a modicum of enthusiasm into her voice, though heaven knew, she didn't feel it. 'Yes, I've been over in Southampton for the day. How about you?'

'Business in London. You know how it is.'

Mrs Frazer claimed the seat Sean had left vacant. Emma shut her book—she hoped without too visible a sigh—and said politely, 'Actually I don't know what it is that you do, Mrs Frazer.'

She only knew the Frazers in passing: they were the couple who had bought Seagulls from her. Though she had met them several times during the viewings and negotiations over price, she hadn't been in a frame of mind then to take much personal interest in them. A glass of sherry, and a few token words of condolence, had just about summed up their relationship.

But grief didn't provide an excuse for self-absorption any more, so she listened first with feigned, then with very real, interest as Mrs Frazer outlined how she and her husband Keith had spent years building up a gift shop business in the North-east. Apparently they had decided to semi-retire on the proceeds—Mrs Frazer was in her fifties, Emma guessed—and to 'keep their hands in' by starting a similar shop on the Island—perhaps in Ryde.

Ryde was not only a popular seaside resort, it was one in which Emma had a minimum of contacts, and no outlet for her work. So her only problem was in toning down her eagerness by the time she had a chance to ask, 'What kind of thing do you plan to sell?'

'Just about anything that takes our fancy,' Mrs Frazer said complacently. 'We're quite interested in——'

But Emma wasn't to know yet what interested her, because the rest of her sentence was drowned by the loudspeaker, announcing that they were about to dock in East Cowes, and ordering car passengers back to their vehicles.

'I'll tell you another time,' Mrs Frazer said, bustling to her feet. 'Come over and see us. If it wouldn't bring back too many unhappy memories. . .?'

'Not at all; I'd love to see what you've done to the house.'

'Ring me and we'll fix a time.'

Which *was* a real proof that the day had turned the corner, Emma decided, as she joined the surge of passengers down the steps to the car deck.

She unlocked the doors of her Volvo, then paused, wondering where Sean had got to. She was at the back of the ferry so it would be a few minutes before she could drive off, but she guessed that even so he'd be quite capable of failing to turn up in time.

In that she had misjudged him, though, because he appeared at that very moment, in the company of the lorry driver he had been talking to earlier.

'Look,' he said, as soon as he reached her side, 'I won't come with you. Shouldn't have asked really, I know nice girls on their own don't take hitch-hikers. Frank will give me a lift in, and show me where to find him in the morning.'

'If you're sure? I was perfectly willing to——'

'Quite sure.' He reached out and caught her face between two cool, long-fingered hands. 'Hey, I'll maybe see you around. Take care, and don't work too hard.' He pulled her gently to him, and just let his mouth brush hers.

She hadn't time to react before he had released her and strode off to join the lorry driver. And, if a few reactions chased through her mind thereafter, they were soon drowned by the much more urgent question of Duncan and his supper. Would he have eaten at Judy's, or would he have insisted on waiting for her?

The latter, she suspected; even if Judy had offered sausages and ice-cream Duncan was perfectly capable of refusing it. A naturally quiet child, inclined to be nervous even with people he knew well, he hated eating away from home. She ought to plan on rustling up something speedy for him: curry from the freezer, maybe.

The ferry emptied rapidly, and only twenty minutes later Emma was making her way through the outskirts of Newport, the Island capital, towards the rambling old house where Judy and her doctor husband Tom lived with their four children.

'Mum!' Duncan yelled, launching himself at her as soon as he had the front door open. 'You've been ages and ages.'

'I know, Dunc, I'm sorry.'

'You said half-past five.'

'True, but I couldn't catch that ferry. Hi, Judy,' she went on, gazing over Duncan's dark head at where Judy, a strikingly tall blonde in khaki dungarees, had just emerged from the kitchen with nine-year old Lucy.

'Good day?' Judy asked, narrowing her eyes as she made her own assessment.

'I've known better, to be honest. Dunc, have you eaten?'

'Just a couple of biscuits to keep him going,' Judy answered.

'Then I'd better get you straight home, lad.'

'You're welcome to have supper here if you like. It'll be potato and leek soup, as soon as Tom's back from surgery.'

'Thanks, but not tonight, Judy.'

'Then call round tomorrow and tell me how it went, OK?'

'I'll do that,' Emma assured her, before repeating her thanks and ushering Duncan to the car.

'You haven't sold much,' Duncan announced, eyeing the heaped-up piles of quilts that filled the back of the estate.

'I'd call that a really helpful remark, Dunc. True Sagittarian tact, as Judy would say.'

Duncan, unabashed, went on, 'Do you have to go back again?'

'I don't know, lovey,' she honestly replied. There *were* a few shopping areas in Southampton that she hadn't tried, but right then she didn't have the stomach to plan a return trip.

'Don't. I don't like it when you go to the mainland without me.'

'Nor do I, Duncan,' Emma wearily agreed.

She swung the Volvo into the narrow street where they lived, and Duncan hopped out of the car to unlock the garage for her.

It wasn't Seagulls, but their new home did have a charm of its own. Once it had been one of the warehouses that overlooked the River Medina, and it had only recently been converted into a modern house. A door from the garage led through a lobby into a small kitchen, beyond which a good-sized living-room made the best of the river views. An open-plan wooden staircase led up to Emma's and Duncan's bedrooms, and another staircase, barely more than a ladder, led up again to the big-beamed loft space that Emma used as a workshop.

Duncan was already hurtling through to the living-room to switch on his home computer. 'Curry?' Emma called after him.

'OK.'

No, she wouldn't unload the Volvo: it could wait till the morning. Instead she switched on the radio, treated herself to a gin and tonic, slid curry into the microwave and put rice to boil on the hob. Then she went to join Duncan in the living-room, and to sit and relax while dinner cooked.

Out on the river, a lone boatman was pottering around in his dinghy. A few gulls swooped and cawed, silhouetted against the red sky. Evening. A time to relax—and although it wasn't easy she did her best to sweep the worries from her mind and do just that.

CHAPTER TWO

'So I really don't know what to do next, Judy,' Emma concluded the second recital of her problems in two days. She was sitting over coffee with her friend in Judy's kitchen, a shabby but cosy room decorated with children's drawings.

Judy frowned. 'Are you desperate for money?'

'Not desperate; not yet. But——'

'I thought not. Taureans never are.'

'Oh, *Judy*.'

Judy raised a silencing hand. 'I was going to add, but they don't often worry without good reason. I'm not underestimating your problems, Em.'

'Maybe I'm *overestimating* them, just a tiny bit. Things get on top of me sometimes. Duncan's sneakers are getting too small, and he needs a new pair of football boots, and two pairs of his school trousers are through at the knees already, and——'

'I know. It's hard being a single mum. Taureans don't figure among the zodiac's happy loners, you know.'

'Marriage didn't suit me much better,' Emma wryly pointed out. 'And self-reliance is a good thing, surely?'

'Finding what's right for *you* is the best thing,' Judy gently corrected her. 'Which means discovering the right balance: not depending entirely on other people, but not turning your back on them either.'

'I know.' She sighed. 'I guess I have become a bit too closed-in recently, but it's helped to share my troubles with you. Thanks.'

'That's what friends are for—although sharing

troubles is only half the answer. Now we need to find you a way forward out of them.'

'I wish I could see one, Jude, but right now I simply can't. I can't imagine being alone forever, but I can't imagine ever marrying again either. I know my work isn't earning me enough, but I'm not qualified to do much else. There just doesn't seem to be a path open to me.'

'You really have sunk low, haven't you?'

She nodded. 'It's hard to find much enthusiasm for life at the moment. When I think back ten years I was so full of optimism, but now it's all turned sour. All I can think now is that I'm twenty-nine, and not young any more. All right,' she hastily continued, seeing the exasperation rise in Judy's face, 'twenty-nine isn't really *old* old, but you have to admit it's an age at which a lot of options seem to close off.'

'Do they?' Judy asked sceptically. 'All right, you're too old to become a fashion model, but that wasn't ever what you wanted, was it?'

'No; true.' Nor did she need reminding that Judy herself was a shining example of a woman who had made good when she was past thirty. Her friend was forty-one now—although she looked ten years younger—and it was only over the previous couple of years that she had successfully turned her hobby of astrology into the basis of a small business.

'But,' she went on, pursuing this line of thought, 'you've got to remember that I've tried self-employment, and it hasn't worked for me.'

'It hasn't failed yet: it's just that it hasn't worked well enough. The trouble is, you're typically Taurean enough to be hung up on security, and you won't relax and fly a kite until you're confident that you won't be dragged off your feet by it.'

'So maybe the answer's to give up the business and find a job working for a big company.'

Judy shook her head. 'I'd hate to see you do that. You'd be lucky to find anything that wasn't run of the mill and badly paid, and a routine clerical job wouldn't solve your cash crisis overnight. Nor can I see you being happy without doing something creative.'

'Nor can I,' Emma agreed. 'That's one good thing about my life—well, two good things. Duncan and quilting.'

'So build on them,' Judy said firmly.

'I'll try. After which, I'd better get back to work on the Log Cabin for the Jacksons. Proof that I do pull in a few commissions, after all!'

'As do I—I've a client coming in at ten-thirty.' Judy glanced at her watch as she got to her feet. 'Keep in touch though, Em,' she said earnestly. 'I like to know what's happening with you, even if it's not all good news. Bring Duncan to tea on Sunday, maybe?'

'We'd love to come.'

Emma's assurance was far more than mere politeness. She needed Judy's friendship—needed to take *and* give more than she had been doing recently, even if it did cost her the occasional hour of her precious working time. All right, Judy couldn't offer magical solutions to her problems, but the knowledge that her friends cared did wonders for her drooping morale.

Her spirits were lighter than they had been for weeks as she set out on the short drive home. It was a glorious day, the autumn sunshine setting a clear sharp edge on the familiar Newport roads. She felt good in her yellow roll-neck sweater and denim dungarees, even if they had both seen better days. And the Log Cabin was one of her favourite patchwork designs, so she could look forward to an enjoyable working session before fetching Duncan from school.

Best to take the short route, then she would get to work all the sooner. She swung the Volvo into a narrow side-road that led towards the harbour, curved around a milk-float—then slammed on the brakes, biting off a curse as she did so. There wasn't usually much traffic along this way, but it was just her luck to pick a moment when another car was roaring at top speed in the opposite direction.

With a squeal of brakes, they managed to stop with six inches between their bumpers. Sighing, Emma slipped into reverse and eased back on to her own side of the road—only to notice that the driver of the other car had climbed out and was bearing down on her.

All right, she'd been in the wrong, but she hadn't actually hit him, so surely he didn't have to make a big thing of it?

Shaken by the narrow escape, furious at her own carelessness, *and* annoyed by the delay, it didn't occur to her till he was a yard off that she recognised both the battered blue Peugeot and its driver—as he did her, to judge by the smile on his face.

This morning Sean was wearing a jumper in blaring stripes of blue and purple, with brown trousers and bright red trainers.

Relief spread a broad grin across her face, as she wound down her window and leaned her head out.

'Morning,' Sean said cheerfully.

'So you got back again.'

'No trouble. Lovely morning, too; I really enjoyed that early crossing.'

'Yes, it's a super day.'

'This your neck of the woods?'

She nodded agreement. 'I live just round the corner.'

'How about a coffee?'

But she'd been meaning to—— Oh, why not? Judy was right, she'd been turning into a killjoy recently, and stonewalling everyone she met wasn't doing any good to her or to them.

'OK,' she agreed. 'You'll need to find somewhere to park: there's only room for my car in my garage. The traffic wardens are red-hot around here, so don't leave your car on the yellow lines. There's some two-hour parking on the quay, or——'

'I've got a garage too.'

'Oh? You mean you live close to here? Or you're staying somewhere. . .? I didn't——'

'I live round the corner too.' He grinned. 'What number are you?'

'Number seven.'

'Number nine's mine. Looks as if I'm your next-door neighbour.'

He'd turned back to his car before she had a chance to react. He glanced at her before getting into it, gestured extravagantly at the corner round which they both lived, then slid into the driver's seat and roared off.

Emma shook her head. Then she eased her car into gear and drove away in a rather more sedate manner.

She was pointing in the right direction and Sean in the wrong one, but by the time she had unlocked her garage, parked, and got out of her car he was standing by the garage door, jingling his car keys.

She hesitated—and that was a mistake, because a dozen conflicting thoughts and feelings came roaring into her head. Pleasure was one of them; and nervousness; and that fear she had felt the day before, when she had realised how easily he had snaked under her defences.

It had been bad enough when she had thought she'd never see him again. But her next-door neighbour. . .!

'This way, is it?' Sean asked, either not noticing or tactfully ignoring her confusion.

'Oh—er—yes. Through here.'

Damn it. She wasn't sixteen any more, so why was she acting so silly at the prospect of giving a man coffee? Especially a man like him, who—all right, he was attractive. Very attractive, even more so than she had thought him yesterday, but so much Neil's type that she couldn't possibly fancy him. Hadn't she been immunised against that sort of man for life?

Obviously not. Anyway, it wasn't his good-natured-salesman manner that had turned her off Neil: she had never really ceased to respond to that side of him. Her love had been destroyed by the weak and selfish nature that lay beneath it. So what she needed to do, she told herself as she led Sean through to her kitchen, was to keep remembering that the appealing exterior was only a front. Behind it, he was doubtless just as much of a disaster zone as Neil had been.

'Couldn't do better, could I?' Sean said with cheerful confidence. 'A lovely lady next door to sew my buttons on for me.'

Yes—how typical.

'And what makes you think I'd do that?'

'Well. . . One, I'll ask you. Two, you're the kind who hates to say no. Three, I always pay favours back.'

'How?'

If he was surprised at her antagonism, he didn't show it. He seemed quite unabashed as he went on, 'That's open to negotiation. I could offer you my services as a car mechanic: I like tinkering with engines. I'm a reasonable carpenter, practised at putting up shelves. I like eating out——'

'I'll settle for a car repair when I need one.'

'Great. Mine's black, two sugars, and if you've any biscuits I'll have a couple of those too.'

'They're in the willow pattern tin on the counter.' What a cheek! she thought. As for his DIY skills, she was willing to bet they'd never be employed on her behalf. Her eyes drifted floorwards and took in the fact that his red trainers had yellow and black striped laces and a hole rubbed right through the left toe. Oh, yes, she knew his type: the charming drifter.

But though he apparently couldn't afford a respectable pair of shoes he *had* paid for three ferry crossings—unless he'd somehow managed to wangle them for free, which she wouldn't have put past him—so she couldn't really begrudge him a couple of biscuits and a coffee.

She heaped coffee into her *cafetière*, poured on boiling water, then turned to watch him munching his way through Duncan's favourite gingernuts, which he did with unselfconscious enthusiasm.

'I noticed number nine had been sold.'

'At last,' Sean agreed, swallowing the last crumbs and wiping his mouth with the back of his hand.

'Oh, I didn't mean to suggest it was a hard-to-sell house. It's not that different from this, is it? I just meant——'

'Emma, I don't give a damn if nobody else in all Newport wanted my house. It suits me perfectly, and that's what matters. And yes, it's pretty similar to this, or at least the kitchen is. You've two floors upstairs?'

'Want to see?' she asked impulsively.

'Of course I do,' Sean agreed.

Leaving the coffee to brew, Emma lead him through to her living-room, where he inspected Duncan's computer games, read the titles on her bookshelf, discussed the tide times with a view to borrowing her dinghy, and asked her opinion of the exhibition showing at the Arts

Centre across the river. Then she took him upstairs, though caution kept her from doing more than half opening the bedroom doors; then finally up again to her workspace.

She had been thinking of a five-minute tour, but Sean wasn't the kind of person with whom anything took five minutes. He was interested in everything, curious about everything. Knowledgeable, too, at least about computer games and books and art exhibitions, though he admitted to being ignorant about patchwork and quilting.

But he was very willing to find out more, so she left him browsing among her heap of finished quilts, her big plastic tubs of fabric and her bales of quilt wadding, and went down to pour their coffees and bring them back upstairs.

When she returned it was to find him flicking through one of her books of quilt patterns.

'So you take the patterns out of here?' he challenged, looking up at her.

'Some of them. My speciality is original designs— although that's not so unusual, it's true of most first-rate professional quilters. Some of them go in for figurative appliqué, but my designs are mainly abstract. Quite a lot of my clients are looking for traditional-style quilts, though, and most of my students are happier starting on those, so I do formal designs from the pattern book about forty per cent of the time. It might sound routine to you,' she finished, suddenly hesitant in case her rush of enthusiasm had bored him, 'but actually there's a lot of artistic judgement involved in choosing the balance of colours and fabric patterns.'

'Obviously there would be. So this design's out of the book?' He gestured at the piece she was doing for the Jacksons. She had finished the patchwork, and had it stretched out on a quilting frame ready for her to tack together the layers of patchwork, wadding and backing.

'In a sense. This kind of pattern, with squares built up out of intersecting oblongs, is called Log Cabin. It's a very famous American design, with lots of classic variations, mainly depending on the balance of dark and light fabrics the quilter uses. I've used a variation called Barn Raising. That gives me the diagonal pattern of lights and darks, then I've planned the internal repetitions myself. See, every third square uses this little-brown-flowered fabric, and every alternate one this white-on-beige, and. . .'

Every element in the complex quilt had been carefully planned, and spurred by Sean's interest she explained it at length, showing him her working diagrams as well as the finished product.

He was so clearly *not* bored that she soon stopped worrying about his reactions, even though she was normally much briefer when talking about her work, even to clients. Eventually she moved on from the Log Cabin quilt to show him a selection of other traditional designs she had in stock, including a few antique quilts as well as ones she had made herself.

Then, since his questions continued to come thick and fast, she showed him two or three of her own-design quilts, explaining how she planned the fabric effects, and how she was learning more about dyeing techniques to help her achieve them.

'It's a really skilled job, isn't it?' Sean said at last.

'It is, yes. There's so much background to learn, and top-level quilting takes years of practice and experience. I've been studying quilt-making since I was thirteen! That's why I'm so keen to carry on making a living at it. When I think of giving all this up, and going to work in a shop or office——'

'You mustn't,' he said firmly.

'I only hope you're right.'

'There must be ways you can build the business up.' He frowned; then looked up and caught her eyes, his familiar grin returning. 'You can make a quilt for me, for starters. I've barely begun to furnish next door.'

'I'd love to, if you're sure you can afford it. I'd better warn you, though, a double-bed size will set you back a couple of hundred pounds at least. Quilts are luxury items, which is one reason why I've had so much trouble finding shops to take them. I do make some smaller pieces like cushions and tea-cosies, but full-size quilts certainly aren't impulse buys.'

'That's OK, I can afford it.' He considered. 'Do me something really good, the best you can. I'd like it to be blue, ideally—and I'm afraid I'd prefer a traditional design. There are lots of quilts I like here, but nothing that's absolutely——'

'I'll happily design one just for you, if you don't mind waiting a few weeks for it,' Emma assured him. Her eyes lingered on him. Blue, yes, to go with those startling eyes of his. She'd enjoy making him a quilt, she thought, and not only because she needed the work: it wasn't often she came across clients as enthusiastic and involving as he was. But even so, the thought of this eccentric scruff buying one of her best custom-designed quilts made her smile.

'How about the Next-Door Neighbour design?' she said thoughtfully.

'Is there one?'

'Oh, yes. Actually I'm rather fond of it; it's a strong design with lots of internal rhythms. Must be in here somewhere. . .'

She picked up the pattern book Sean had discarded, and leafed through it rapidly. 'Here it is. Do you like that? In a mixture of blues, perhaps with a little white or cream mixed in?'

'Looks good. Shall I pay you now?'

'Well, I—no, of course not. I normally ask for payment when clients have approved my working designs.'

'Fair enough.'

Yes—fair enough. So why did she feel irritated? Because it had struck her that he was humouring her, that was why! His show of interest had had her so thoroughly fooled that she'd almost forgotten her earlier admission to him that she was broke and desperate.

All of which she would never have admitted, she thought awkwardly, if she had had an inkling that he was going to be a neighbour of hers. Sympathy from friends was one thing, but charity from virtual strangers was another, and she didn't want it!

Obviously he didn't really want a quilt. Just as obviously, he'd be hard pressed to afford one. In fact it was quite possible, she thought viciously, her eyes on those disreputable trainers, that he emphatically *couldn't* afford it, and was fooling himself as well as her. That she could well believe: Neil had done the same thing often enough, vaguely intending to help friends while actually causing them endless hassle and upset and expense.

She could hardly accuse him straight out of leading her on over the quilt, but she did make a silent resolution that she wouldn't make it for him. Probably he didn't really expect her to, anyway.

'Hey,' Sean said, getting to his feet, then gingerly rubbing his head where he'd knocked it against one of the low beams, 'it's past one o'clock. Share a sandwich at the pub with me, and then I'd better be getting back. I've some work to do myself.'

'The pub's a bit expensive. We can have a sandwich here.'

'No, I was offering to treat you. And don't think up more excuses; it won't take us long.'

'All right. Just give me a minute to run a comb through my hair.'

'Women,' Sean groaned. But she wasn't braving the lunchtime crowd in the Wheatsheaf in her working clothes, and it only took her five minutes to swap the dungarees for a narrow-ribbed red jumper and dark brown corduroy skirt, to slick on a little brown eye-shadow, and to give her hair the promised once-over.

He appreciated this effort, to judge from the gleam in his eyes when she rejoined him. And, though she couldn't help feeling wary, Emma did relish his approval. Her life had been so low-key recently that a lunchtime sandwich in a pub rated as a treat, and it lifted her spirits to walk through the town in the company of a tall, good-looking man, even if he was dressed like an extra from *The Wizard of Oz*.

The Wheatsheaf, only five minutes' walk away, was one of the busiest of Newport's town centre pubs. Emma hadn't called in for months, but she wasn't surprised to find a sprinkling of familiar faces in the saloon bar; in a small town like Newport, everybody tended to know everybody else. She recognised Dave Madison, a local dentist and father of Duncan's friend Ben, sitting in a corner with his partner Bill Caxton; her accountant, Phil Hargreaves, propping up the bar, and several other acquaintances.

She hadn't much option but to pause and say hello to all these people, and to introduce Sean to them. Fortunately it was a pleasure to introduce Sean, since he was the kind of easygoing extrovert who managed to give

everyone the impression that he was delighted to meet
them.

Which he was, perhaps, because although it took them
ages to reach the bar, there was no hint of annoyance in
his voice when he commented to her, 'I didn't realise
this was a regular haunt of yours.'

'Actually it's not, but I doubt if I could go anywhere
in Newport without meeting someone I knew.'

'Do you like that?'

'Of course! Wouldn't anyone?'

'Not necessarily,' he said thoughtfully. 'To a
Londoner like me it seems strange; even a bit claustro-
phobic, to think you can't have a quiet drink and a
sandwich without everyone in town knowing about it.'

'That's true. You can't keep much secret on the
Island.'

'So which of your friends shall we join?'

She hadn't been intending them to join anyone! To
say hello, yes; but with the greetings over she had
expected to have Sean to herself, and to ask him some
questions in retaliation for his morning's pumping of
her.

What? she thought, appalled, recognising her own
idiocy. Hadn't she already decided Sean was the most
dangerously attractive route to disaster she had met since
Neil? So what was she doing craving intimate tête-à-têtes
with him? Joining Ted and Marie Morland, who were
waving frantically from their table by the window, would
be infinitely more sensible, even if it hadn't been what
Sean himself intended.

'Over there,' she said tersely.

Marie, a plump, cheerful woman in her thirties, was
one of the students in Emma's evening quilting class, as
she wasted no time in telling Sean. She worked in a

newsagent's in the town centre, and her husband Ted, quiet and balding, was an insurance broker.

'I don't know yet what you do, Sean,' Emma managed to put in, once the introductions were complete. At least she was determined to find out that much!

Sean shrugged. 'This and that. I do quite a bit of writing, but I get bored if I do it all the time. So I have a stake in a friend's restaurant back in London, and I act as a small-scale literary agent, and. . .all sorts of things.'

'Jack of all trades,' Marie suggested.

'I've been called that before,' he agreed.

'What do you write?' Ted asked. 'Books? Articles?'

'Mainly books, though I do a few articles on sailing.'

'So you're published? You're well known?'

'I'm not a household name exactly, but I make a living out of it.'

'What's your name?' Marie persisted. 'Your writing name?'

'Sean Davies. I use that name for my fiction: the "Silas South" detective novels. The sailing articles I do as S. M. Davies, since I like to keep them separate.'

'Sounds marvellous,' Marie enthused.

Yes, it did, Emma reluctantly acknowledged. Writing was a glamorous job—at least from the outside—and those casual mentions of whole series of books would impress anyone. Unless they were reading between the lines, and then. . .

The manner in which Sean had spoken, expansive but vague, was so horribly familiar to her. It was just the way Neil had always talked. He'd always been full of 'business ventures' and 'marvellous opportunities', and his slick, enthusiastic manner had conned plenty of outsiders into believing he was a successful businessman. But when you shared his life as Emma had done you discovered the reality behind the euphemisms. The

A DESIRE TO LOVE

'ventures' were usually no more than some half-baked scheme he'd cooked up with a couple of mates in the pub one night.

Sean was certainly right in saying he wasn't a household name. Admittedly detective novels weren't her thing, but even so she could have named the top handful of writers, and she felt sure Sean Davies wasn't one of them. As for 'having a stake in a friend's restaurant'—couldn't that be a roundabout way of saying he'd worked as a waiter when times were tough?

She didn't suspect him of direct lying. Quite likely he'd had the odd book published; he certainly looked like an author. A struggling author! It was just that his manner hinted at mock-modesty, at something grander, which she didn't believe to be justified. After all, how could a man with a car like his, *and* holey trainers, seriously expect to pass himself off as a success in life?

Even his house. . . OK, it was a nice house, very similar to hers, but it was a *small* nice house—and in a part of the country that was very much cheaper than the better areas of London. Writers who were making it big in London literary circles didn't generally up sticks and move to Newport, Isle of Wight!

Oh, yes, she thought, she would definitely be wise to forget about his quilt commission.

'Sean, you'll have another? And you, Emma?' Ted enquired, picking up their empty lager and tomato-juice glasses.

'Thanks, Ted, mine's a half of lager,' Sean agreed.

'I won't, if you don't mind,' Emma said quietly. 'I've really got to get back and do some work now. I'll see you on Thursday, Marie.'

'If you can hang on for ten minutes I'll walk you back,' Sean offered.

Emma shook her head. She guessed his ten minutes

were all too likely to turn into half an hour or longer, and, while he might not care about getting any work done that afternoon, she didn't feel the same way.

As she weaved her way out of the crowded bar she could see him leaning over, hands waving, in earnest conversation with Marie, and looking as if he was settled until mid-afternoon at least.

In fact it proved to be well worth while for Emma to get back quickly, because only a few minutes after her return she had a phone call from Mrs Frazer, inviting her to tea.

Her only regret was that she had already arranged tea with Judy for that Sunday, so she had to postpone this invitation until the following week. No problem, Mrs Frazer assured her, and they rang off with an arrangement for three o'clock on Sunday week confirmed.

With her mind on the planned gift shop in Ryde, Emma was looking forward to the visit; but Duncan's reaction, when he came back from his friend Tony's at five-thirty, was a loud, 'Oh, Mum!'

'All right, Dunc,' she sighed. 'I know you're not crazy about having tea with grown-ups, but I need to go, so it's not negotiable. Anyway, I expect the Frazers will let you play on the beach, and you'll enjoy that, won't you?'

'Will they? Honestly?'

His naïve enthusiasm made her heart sink further. It hadn't been wise to mention the possiblity in case the Frazers *didn't* allow it; and it hurt her, to see how much Duncan still missed Seagulls. There were many worse places to bring up a boy than Newport harbour, but they didn't have any garden any more, let alone their own stretch of beach, and she hated having deprived him of so much.

'I'll definitely ask them,' she assured him, glancing at

her watch. 'Supper in ten minutes. Then I'll have a game of chess with you if you like, and after that I'm afraid I'll have to work while you read or watch television till bedtime.'

'I bet I'll beat you today.'

It wasn't a long-odds bet: Emma was tired, and Duncan was a bright child, whose chess game was already a good match for hers. It wouldn't be long before he always beat her, and needed to look around for more demanding opponents.

Neil had been a better match for him—and, though he had been an erratic father, when he was in the mood the two of them had spent hours playing together. Duncan didn't have that any more, either. She bit down hard on the thought, and went to fetch the board.

When Duncan's neat fork trapped her queen a couple of dozen moves into the game she was ready to resign, but in spite of her offer of a second game Duncan was still young enough to want to rub in his victories. He insisted that she play on, and she was doing her best to sustain her interest when the doorbell rang.

It gave her a little jolt to see Sean waiting on the doorstep. 'It's not your suppertime?' he asked, before slipping past her into the lobby.

'No, Duncan and I are playing chess.'

'I brought over a couple of books on design that I thought you might like,' he offered, holding them out. 'Give you some ideas—although it doesn't strike me you're short of those.'

'I'm always looking for more,' Emma assured him. She took the books from him, and gave them a quick flick-through, uneasily conscious of his tall figure, close to her in the narrow hallway, and of his eyes on her.

The books were both heavily illustrated, one about Celtic patterns, the other on Arabic design. There was a definite resemblance between the intricate, colourful patterns and those of patchwork quilts, and there was real enthusiasm in her voice as she thanked Sean for his thoughtfulness.

'Can I beg a quick coffee?' he asked. 'I won't be interrupting you for too long, because I've booked myself for the darts team at the Wheatsheaf tonight.'

'That was fast work.'

'It was, actually; I can't have stayed more than a quarter of an hour after you left. I got some good work done this afternoon, too.'

Oh yes? she thought sceptically. But she led him through and introduced him to Duncan, before making her chess move, then retreating to the kitchen to brew the coffee.

'You're losing,' Sean announced when she returned.

'Thank you, but I know that already.'

'If you wrap up this game fast, Duncan, I'll just have time to play you myself. If you'd like that. . .?'

Emma bit her lip, praying Duncan wouldn't refuse too rudely. Knowing how awkward he could be with strangers, she didn't dare to hope he'd agree. But in fact he nodded curtly, and gestured to Emma to overturn her king and admit defeat.

She reclaimed her chair and watched while Duncan and Sean set the board up again, and began to play. Sean seemed very competent. He chatted away, outlining the strengths and weaknesses of the opening he was following; but he wasn't patronising about his knowledge, and he praised Duncan enthusiastically when the boy made a thoughtful move.

Those startling light blue eyes of his flickered to hers while Duncan was focusing on the board, and she thought she read from them a promise to pitch his game so that Duncan wasn't completely outplayed. That pleased her: she liked it no more than Duncan did when well-meaning adults clumsily 'threw' games, but a subtle handicapping never came amiss.

Duncan was a pawn up, though his remaining pieces were in less good positions than Sean's, when Emma slipped away, carrying her coffee up to her workroom. She switched on the powerful light that hung low over the quilting frame, retrieved her tacking thread and needle, and got back to work tacking the Log Cabin quilt together.

Normally she played music while she quilted, but this time she didn't switch on her little stereo, wanting to keep an ear open for Duncan and Sean. There was no sound from downstairs, though, and soon she became fully absorbed in the work.

'Time to stop.'

The low voice, coming from just behind her left shoulder, made her jump and drop the needle.

'Sorry,' Sean said, moving closer. 'I would have thumped up the stairs, but that's not easy in trainers. How's it going?'

'Steadily.'

'Do you work every evening?'

'Every other evening, more or less. I usually leave it till Duncan's in bed, but——'

'I took up lots of your time this morning, didn't I? I'll find a way to make it up. Anyway, Duncan just won that game—he's a good little player—and it's time I was off.'

'I'll come down and see you out.'

'There's no need.'

'I've got to get Duncan to bed soon, anyway.' She got to her feet.

Sean was standing between her and the head of the stairs, and she paused, waiting for him to move. But he didn't; he just stood there, holding her gaze, until her awareness of him had reached a fine pitch of acuteness.

Her attic workroom was low-roofed, with thick wooden beams running across it. That morning, in daylight, she hadn't really been aware of how Sean filled it, but now, with the shadow thrown from the low lamp stretching out behind him, he looked huge.

His figure wasn't menacing, but it was emphatically masculine—unexpectedly so in a way, because he wasn't remotely the macho type. It occurred to her that she hadn't invited any other men up here. Her quilt classes contained only women.

'Do you get lonely?' Sean asked suddenly.

She bridled instantly. 'Not in that sense!'

'What sense? Oh,' he went on, answering his own question, 'I wasn't making a pass, I meant it literally. I was just thinking, all those evenings alone. . .'

'I don't really mind them.' She moved a step closer to the stairs, half wanting to break the mood that was holding them, half wanting to stay and talk. 'At least, when I'm quilting I don't. Of course it's a lonely life being a single parent: nobody could deny that. But I'd have to spend most of my evenings alone in the house in any case, and it's a pleasure, really, to have something to do to fill them.'

'I can see that.'

'Mum!' Duncan called from down the stairs.

'Just coming,' she shouted back, before turning once more to Sean. 'It's lonelier for Duncan, if anything,' she went on. 'It was nice of you to stop and play with him. Thank you.'

'Any time.' Sean gestured her to the stairs. 'That's assuming you don't mind me calling in. . .?'

'Not at all,' she said automatically. Then hesitated, because in truth she wasn't sure if she did mind. He had

an unnerving effect on her. She hadn't really been aware
of men since Neil's death, and certainly hadn't felt any
inclination to look for a replacement for him, but she
could feel her nerve-ends tingling with awareness whenever Sean moved close to her. Even the sight of him,
standing casually across the room, was enough to induce
that half-forgotten tug of attraction inside her.

If he was to keep on calling round like this, she
thought uneasily, she might find it hard to keep on
holding him at arm's length.

But she couldn't have explained that to him, so she
hurried downstairs to see what Duncan wanted; and a
minute later Sean had gone, and she was shepherding
Duncan towards the bathroom.

CHAPTER THREE

'DUNCAN! Duncan!'

Emma's voice rose as she hurried down the steep slope that formed the lower half of the garden at Seagulls. This lovely place was also dangerous, and there had always been a moment, going after Neil and Duncan down on the shore, when she had felt a terror that something might have happened to them.

'Duncan!' she shouted louder still. 'Where are you?'

'Down here, Mum.' Duncan's dark head emerged from behind a tangle of brambles, and she breathed out a sigh of relief.

'Hang on,' she called irritably. 'I haven't got the right shoes on.'

'Take them off,' Duncan offered.

'I can't do that, we've got to go back up in a minute.' She glanced down at her black high-heeled court shoes and blue woollen dress, then back up the rough path.

'You never used to wear clothes like that to come to the beach,' Duncan grumbled.

'There never used to be Mr and Mrs Frazer in the house to be polite to,' Emma retorted acidly.

She had dressed up for them, guessing them to be the kind of people who would notice; and they were, to judge from Mrs Frazer's—Rose's—smart maroon two-piece and diamond brooch. Even so, the visit had caught her off balance: what she hadn't bargained for was the effect that seeing what they had done to Seagulls would have on her.

Of course she had regretted leaving the lovely clifftop

46

house, for Duncan's sake even more than for her own. But at the time—and for much of the time since—she had played down that feeling, telling herself that it was better for them both to be in the town centre, where there were other children for Duncan to play with, and other single-parent families.

In much the same way she had played down her regret at Neil's death, she thought with a kind of shame. She reminded herself regularly about the rows they used to have, the times when they couldn't pay the bills, the horrible uncertainty when Neil had been 'between jobs'; but she didn't let herself think nearly as often about the golden afternoons they had spent down here, picnicking on crabs and lemonade, creating hideaways for Duncan among the bushes; even just sitting, arm in arm, and gazing out to sea.

It had been a defence mechanism, she supposed: a way of coping with the pain. She had needed to persuade herself that there were advantages to her new life. But now, coming back to the house she had loved so much and finding it changed beyond recognition, the pangs of loss were piercingly strong.

Neil had shared her own tastes in décor, and together they had taken endless trouble over Seagulls. The huge sitting-room overlooking the sea they had decorated in shades of sea-green, graduating from almost white on the ceiling to a deep aqua in the alcoves and on the wood-work. It had been a light, welcoming room, with cheap but comfortable cane-framed armchairs and sofas stuffed with flowered cushions.

The Frazers had repainted it the most ghastly sugar-pink, and filled the alcoves with ugly knick-knacks. Their chairs were hard and spindly, and they were even talking of ripping out the Victorian cast-iron fireplace and replacing it with a flame-effect gas fire.

Their furnishings were more luxurious than Emma's and Neil's had been, but ugly, ugly! The old Seagulls had gone, swept away under a tide of bric-à-brac and gold fringing. It hurt her to see it.

Although it was no better really coming down here, where the Frazers hadn't made any changes at all, and realising that Neil was never going to clamber over the stones again, never going to make the tree-house he'd planned with Duncan, never going to stretch out on the rough grass in the sunshine and pretend to read a thriller before falling asleep.

'I wish we hadn't come,' Duncan said in a small voice.

Emma turned to him guiltily. Wrapped up in her own thoughts, she hadn't really taken it in that this return was just as bad for him. Worse, perhaps, because while she had seen Neil's faults only too clearly, Duncan had adored his daddy unreservedly.

She reached out her arms, and Duncan clambered the couple of yards that separated them, and came to her for an awkward hug.

'Thinking about Daddy?'

Duncan nodded.

'So was I.'

'I don't like those people,' Duncan said in a small but firm voice.

'Nor do I much, lovey. But we've got to be polite now we've come, and there's still a possibility they'll agree to sell some of my work in this gift shop they're talking about.'

'Do we have to stay much longer?'

Emma shook her head. 'We'll just go up for a few more minutes. You tell them you had a lovely time down here, then we'll thank them for asking us and be on our way.'

'I hope we don't have to come again.'

'So do I.'

Duncan held her hand as they slowly retraced their steps. Up the steep rough path, on to the level terrace with its apple and plum trees, across the sloping lawns, and through the open french windows into that hateful sitting-room.

'Been having fun, young man?' asked Keith Frazer, a large, plump, red-faced man.

Duncan nodded nervously.

'I'll tell you what, I've found you a treat.'

Emma pushed him forward, and Mr Frazer produced from behind his back a yellow lollipop.

Perhaps it was the force of Emma willing it that made Duncan bring out a tentative 'thanks'. All right, it was a babyish thing to give him, but the Frazers obviously weren't used to children, and must have meant well.

'We've been talking while you and your mum were down on the beach,' Mr Frazer went on, 'and we've got something to offer her too.'

'I really don't——'

'Not a lollipop,' Mrs Frazer said with a little giggle.

'Oh, no. We've a proposition for you, Emma. We'd like to sell your quilts in our gift shop.'

'Now we won't mess up any arrangements you've already made,' Mrs Frazer assured her, taking over the conversation, 'or your private commissions either. But if you make sixty quilts a year, then I reckon we can take forty of them.'

'Forty!'

'And most of your cushions too.'

'But you haven't even seen my work!'

'Of course we have, dear,' Mrs Frazer assured her. 'We saw it when we first looked round the house.'

Ye-es. Of course everybody who had looked around Seagulls had noticed her workroom, and admired the quilts draped on every bed and hung on the dining-room walls; but she couldn't remember the Frazers showing any more than the usual level of interest. That they should offer to take forty quilts, on no better basis than that, astonished her.

'It'll have to be something like normal trade terms,' Mr Frazer went on. 'We know you're on your own, and we wouldn't want to be too hard, but we're no charity, you'll understand. Let's say, thirty per cent commission on sales?'

Thirty per cent! That was astonishing too—astonishingly good! She had set the Frazers down for hard bargainers, but those were more than reasonable terms. Her last sale had been to a craft shop in Portsmouth which had taken only two quilts, and demanded fifty per cent commission.

But though this was what she had hoped for—and more—it seemed almost too good, coming from these people whom she frankly didn't like. Cautiously, she couldn't help feeling around for drawbacks.

'It's the winter season coming up. I mean, it's hardly the ideal time for selling. . .'

'Nonsense—quilts make a great Christmas present, and there's still quite a bit of tourist trade,' Rose Frazer said confidently. 'We're reckoning to open up in November, settle into the Christmas rush, then tick over till the spring. I take it you've some work in stock?'

'Quite a lot, yes. Of course, I need to keep some quilts in my collection: there are the classes to think about, and my private customers. But I could let you have——' she calculated rapidly '—probably twenty before Christmas. One or two could be the hand-quilted ones, which come more expensive, and the rest would be machine-sewn.'

'That'd do fine. Now what do you say to a glass of sherry? We'll drink to our deal.'

Going home, a sherry and another cup of tea later—not to mention much surreptitious foot-shuffling by Duncan—Emma and Duncan had a good row in the car.

'Oh, for heaven's sake!' Emma finally exploded. 'I know you don't want to go back there, Dunc, and nor do I, but it's such a good deal that I couldn't possibly have refused it. If the Frazers will help us pay our bills we'll just have to learn to like them.'

'I'll never like them,' Duncan said mutinously.

'You mustn't judge by appearances, Dunc. Sometimes people you don't like the look of turn out to be the kindest of all.'

'Some don't.'

'But the Frazers have! That's the point, they've offered me the one thing I needed more than anything! Hey, we can celebrate tonight. Takeaway Chinese with spare ribs?'

'Yes!' For once Duncan's face lit up with pleasure. 'Sean likes spare ribs too.'

'So?'

That was no news to Emma. Sean had bought them a takeaway the week before, and thrown in double portions of ribs, one barbecued, one sweet and sour, half of which he had devoured himself. But if Duncan was suggesting they knock him up and invite him over, then her enthusiasm was muted, to put it kindly.

After all, neither she nor Duncan had seen Sean since that Chinese meal. For a few days he had practically lived in their house, calling round once or twice each day, then he had disappeared without a word.

He had gone away, she assumed, since she hadn't encountered him on the street or noticed any lights lit in number nine. But he might have said something first! It was surely only natural that she and Duncan should have felt first bewildered, then concerned, and finally rather angry at his sudden defection.

'Shall we ask if he wants to come and get some with us?' Duncan persisted.

'I doubt if he's there, Dunc.'

'We can knock and see.'

'If you like, but I shouldn't bank on him answering.'

Duncan did ring Sean's bell for several minutes, but Emma was right: there wasn't any reply, or any sign that his house was inhabited.

'Forget it, love,' she urged. 'We can have a nice celebration on our own.' But Duncan's face told her that it would be second-best for there to be just the two of them.

He did like having a man in the house. A father-figure, she thought sadly, recalling their brief talk about Neil that afternoon. Sean had made no attempt to become more than a friend to her, but he'd done a great job with his daddy-substitute act.

So? Sean wasn't the only man in the world, and if Duncan's open enthusiasm for him when he was around had threatened to become embarrassing, his pining for him now that he'd gone was much more so. Maybe the answer was to introduce a new daddy-substitute?

Trouble was, the ideal daddy-substitute would have to be a man she was prepared to consider as a husband— and she didn't much fancy any of the available men she knew.

But then, Sean himself didn't rate in her book as suitable husband material, so she could hardly pretend that—that Dave Madison, say, would be a worse choice.

In fact, when she thought about it, Dave might be a good choice. It was six months since Alison had left him, but he wasn't seeing anyone else, as far as she knew. His son Ben was a friend of Duncan's, and Dave himself was—OK, a little overbearing, she'd always thought, but wasn't it worth giving him a chance? She felt reasonably sure he'd welcome an invitation—he'd asked her out a couple of times recently, only to get stalling replies—and it was always possible he'd come to seem less overbearing on better acquaintance.

'I'll tell you what we could do,' she said slowly. 'We could ring the Madisons, and see if Ben's staying with his dad today. Maybe if he is, they could both come over.'

'Yeah!' Duncan said eagerly.

'I'll do that now.'

Her luck was in: Dave did have Ben with him for the day, and didn't have to return him to his mother until eight o'clock. He was almost embarrassingly keen to take up the invitation, and promised to turn up in half an hour, after picking up the takeway en route.

'What's this I hear,' Judy demanded over the phone on Monday afternoon, 'about you going out with Dave Madison?'

'Now how on earth did that get back to you?'

'Through Lucy, who got it from Duncan.'

Emma gritted her teeth. 'I didn't mean it to be broadcast all over town. Anyway, it wasn't "going out"— we only shared a takeaway.'

'Come over—I want to talk about it. I'll do you a reading, too.'

'I can't come in working hours,' Emma demurred.

'After school, then. Tomorrow?'

Emma sighed. 'OK, I'll see you then.'

* * *

No sooner had Duncan been banished to Judy's garden on Tuesday afternoon, with Lucy and eleven-year-old Donald, than Judy came out with, 'Didn't I warn you about Aries men?'

'Dave, you mean?'

'Dave.'

'I didn't know he was. All right, don't tell me: they're a disastrous combination with Taurus women.'

'Absolutely horrendous.'

'Maybe there's something else in his chart that explains it. Some special aspect that——'

'But you don't even like him, Em!'

'Now that's not fair,' Emma protested. 'Neil and I used to see a lot of Dave and Alison, and we always got on fine.'

'That's different.' Judy sighed. 'I know. You're lonely, and Dave's presentable and well off and not bad company in his way. But he's the kind of man who'd tread all over you, honestly.'

'Maybe you're right. But I feel I ought to give it a try, if only for Duncan's sake.'

Judy scowled, then gestured to her to sit down at the kitchen table. 'You've got an interesting chart at the moment,' she announced. 'Everything's happening in your life, all of a sudden. You might think you had enough of an upheaval last year, but there's more yet to come.'

'Oh no!'

'Why? Are you happy at the moment?'

'Not really.' Emma considered this prediction, then said slowly, 'You're probably right. In a way, I've been in a period of transition for the last year. Things have changed, changed a lot, but I haven't had my working life sorted out, and I haven't got my love-life sorted out either. More than anything, I've been waiting to recover; waiting till I was ready to start again.'

'Recover from Neil? And are you?'

'It's coming,' she said with quiet confidence. 'I've just about got to the point where I can bear to think back on it all. Dunc and I went back to Seagulls the other day, and. . .'

She outlined to Judy, as honestly as she could, her thoughts and feelings on that Sunday afternoon, then went on, 'I'm beginning to think you were right, Jude, when you told me I wouldn't make a loner. But I don't have any experience of happy marriage, and when I ask myself what kind of man I should get involved with now it's difficult to see how anyone short of Superman could fit the bill.'

'Don't choose Superman: flying isn't for you,' Judy snappily retorted. 'How about your parents—don't they provide you with a role model?'

'They're happy,' Emma agreed. 'But my mother's totally different from me. She's an Aries, as it happens! And though I love my father dearly I can't imagine marrying a man remotely like him.'

Judy frowned. 'It's hard to know what to say, Em. Astrology isn't an exact science, and maybe I am wrong in warning you off Dave. I can point out the danger areas, but the bottom line is that you have to follow your own instincts, make your own choices.'

'Is there much love interest in my chart?'

'Oh, yes—it's very strong. I'd be surprised if you didn't meet someone who set your heart fluttering this autumn.'

'The odd flutter's hardly what I'm looking for.'

'Now why do you say that?' Judy queried. 'Not all love-affairs start off in deadly earnest, you know! Or does it have something to do with that new neighbour of yours?'

'Sean Davies?' To Emma's annoyance, she felt herself turning red, and she knew her air of nonchalance wasn't very convincing as she said offhandedly, 'Oh, there's nothing doing there.'

'Why not?'

'He's not the type. Or rather, he's the Neil type, and I've had enough of those to last me several lifetimes already.'

Judy slowly shook her head. 'Not so, Em. Neil was a Gemini, and Sean's an Aquarian.'

'I thought you hadn't met him?'

'I haven't, but I've heard plenty about him.'

'From people who asked him when his birthday was?'

'I am a pro!' Judy retorted, mock-hurt. 'All right, I'm only ninety-nine per cent certain. But you ask him, and I bet I'll be proved right.'

'I wouldn't take you on there,' Emma assured her. Some of Judy's confidence in astrology she couldn't share, but on this level she didn't doubt her friend's competence. 'So what does Aquarius signify?'

'Well, it's an air sign, ruled by Uranus, the planet of unpredictability.'

'That's Sean.'

'They're charming, imaginative people. A little way-out, but not as unworldly as they look. Interested in everything and everybody—and sometimes rather hard to tie down to one particular person.'

'A lousy match for me, in other words.'

'Not always,' Judy said thoughtfully. 'Some astrologers claim that Aquarians never fall for Taureans, though there are more than a few Taureans who wish they would. They tend to find Taureans dull and stolid;

they underestimate them, in some ways. And, not surprisingly, the Taureans don't appreciate that! But artistic
Taureans—and there are plenty of those—often appeal
to Aquarians. It would take a blind man to think you
unimaginative, and Aquarians aren't blind!'

'True,' Emma slowly agreed. 'I don't have Sean's kind
of imagination, though. He's what you'd call a kite-flyer,
Jude. I've been designing quilts for sixteen years, and in
a week he threw me a dozen ideas that I'd never, ever
have come up with by myself.'

'So doesn't that make him good for you?'

'If he were around, he might be.'

'Isn't he?'

She shook her head. 'OK, for a while he was everywhere I looked, in *and* out of my house; but that ended
ten days ago.'

'That's typical. He's not a man who'll stick to a woman
like glue. You have to play that sort in like a fish, and
with a long, long line.'

'And when I get him there? It's all right you saying I
shouldn't take him to be exactly like Neil, but Jude, he's
hardly the soul of stability. I couldn't cope with his
"here today, gone tomorrow" attitude in a long
relationship.'

'Maybe. Give it time, and we'll see.' Judy shrugged
cheerfully, and rose to pour some more coffee. 'Anyway,
there's nothing more either friends or astrology can tell
you right now about your love-life. Let's have a look at
your work instead.'

'Now there the news *is* good,' Emma assured her.

'Is it?'

But Judy's faint scepticism didn't hold up against
Emma's good news about the new gift shop, and soon
the two of them were toasting the Frazers in cooling
coffee, with as much enthusiasm as if it had been
champagne.

CHAPTER FOUR

A COUPLE of days later Rose Frazer called on Emma. Emma had already sorted out a pile of quilts for her, and to her relief after a brief flick-through Rose announced that they would suit her fine.

'I'll set them on one side,' Emma assured her, 'and as soon as the shop opens I'll deliver them to you. Or is it open already?'

'Not yet; we're still sorting out the final details, but I'd rather take them with me now.'

'Are you sure?'

'Quite sure. We're using the attic at Seagulls as storage space for our stock, so I'll leave them up there.'

It was a suitable space: clean, airy and dry, as Emma well knew. She was rather sorry to think of the quilts being stored away where nobody would see them, but Mrs Frazer's plan made sense, and she didn't want to jeopardise their arrangement by questioning it.

She had already made out a list of the quilts in the pile, and Rose willingly agreed to sign it as a receipt.

'Fine,' she said, handing the paper back. 'I've brought our van over, so I'll bring it round from the car park and load them up now.'

'Is there anything we've forgotten?' Emma wondered out loud. 'The selling price I've marked—there's a swing label on each quilt. I'm not VAT-registered myself, but you'll obviously need to add the tax on. And you'll account to me at the end of each month? That's the usual arrangement I've made.'

'That sounds reasonable.'

Emma took a final wistful look at the pile. She had never let anybody take away so many quilts before—and without paying in advance. She couldn't have asked for a deposit, though, when the Frazers' terms were so reasonable, and she couldn't think of anything that might go wrong.

Insurance? She raised that question, and was assured that Rose had already seen to it.

Really it had gone amazingly smoothly, she thought, as Mrs Frazer drove off less than an hour later in her laden van. Emma made herself a cup of coffee, and since there were still twenty minutes until Duncan came back from school she took it upstairs, put Beethoven's Sixth Symphony on the stereo, and set to work planning out a new quilt based on one of the patterns from Sean's book on Arabic design.

That evening was her regular Thursday quilt class. It started at seven-thirty, and as all her pupils were normally very punctual Emma was taken aback when the doorbell went at six-thirty.

Marie Morland quickly stepped in out of the rain, lowering a large red umbrella.

'I've just been to the exhibition opening at the Arts Centre,' she announced.

'Oh? Is it a good exhibition?'

'Smashing. A couple of painters from London; it's one of the best they've done, I think. I was just saying to Ted that you ought to be there. He reminded me you've got to think of Duncan, so I thought, I've seen it all now, so I'll see if Emma'd like to nip over while I keep an eye on him.'

'That's awfully kind of you, Marie.'

'You've had supper?'

'Yes, but I don't normally like to leave Dunc——'

'You go, Mum,' Duncan piped up.

'You wouldn't mind, love? Just for half an hour?'

'He'll be fine with me,' Marie firmly assured her. 'Now set off right away, or you won't have time to see everything.'

Seeing the justice of that, Emma resisted the temptation to dash upstairs and tidy herself. If her jeans, cream shirt and Paisley-quilted jerkin were all right for the quilting class, they would surely do for the friends she was likely to meet at the Arts Centre.

She quickly slipped on her PVC mac, grabbed her own umbrella, and with a few orders to Duncan—who seemed perfectly happy watching television—she dashed out into the rain.

She had been receiving invitations to the Arts Centre openings ever since she had exhibited some of her own work there, but since she had to watch her baby-sitting budget it was a rare treat actually to make one of them. Several friends remarked on how nice it was to see her, as she made her way up the broad stairs to the upstairs gallery, paused to pick up a glass of wine, then looked around for Ted, meaning to thank him for his and Marie's kind thought.

Her eyes slipped around the high brick walls with their brightly coloured canvases, then came to an abrupt halt.

Sean was there.

He was standing at the far side of the room. He was wearing a smart and well-fitting grey suit, and his hair had been cropped to a tamer style and more conventional length. The effect was only marginally spoiled by the fact that he still had on his red trainers; it gave his appearance an eccentric flavour, but even so he looked remarkably—no, presentable wasn't the right word—devastating was closer to the mark. There was a charisma about him, a tigerish energy, which made everybody else in the room seem half alive by comparison.

He had a glass of wine in one hand—with which he was gesturing dangerously—and the other was resting on the shoulder of a small, slim girl with a stunning mane of blonde hair.

Oh. She should have guessed, she supposed, that that was the kind of reason that would keep him from home and work for the best part of a fortnight.

But she hadn't guessed that he would be at the opening—and she minded. She minded seeing him unexpectedly. She minded his invading her little world, and making her feel uncomfortable within it. Most of all, though she hated to admit it to herself, she minded seeing him with a petite and pretty blonde.

So what? she told herself firmly. Just about any attractive man in his thirties, however rackety, had *some* kind of woman in his life. Sean was hardly likely to be the sole exception. He'd never suggested to her that he was available, and, come to that, she'd never suggested that she wished he was—which she hadn't, anyway.

It was stupid, plain stupid, to react as if Sean had thrown her over for the blonde. She and he hadn't been even slightly involved in a romantic way, and for all she knew the blonde girl might have been his regular girl-friend for years.

But, to be fair, he *had* dropped her and Duncan, and without a word of explanation, and she could hardly be blamed for bridling a bit when she found out that this was the reason why.

Maybe she herself ought to know better than to be wounded by that sort of thoughtlessness, but Duncan couldn't be expected to, she thought irritably. Now what was she supposed to do? Pretend to ignore him, or go over and ask to be introduced to the blonde? Common sense said the latter, but the prospect induced an unpleasantly hollow feeling in the pit of her stomach.

Luckily her dilemma solved itself, since Peter Wilson, a friend who was on the Centre committee, came up just then to say hello, and drew her into his circle of friends. She chatted with them for ten minutes, then when the circle broke up she used the opportunity to take a better look at the pictures. Peter stayed by her side and they drifted round the gallery, discussing the exhibition.

Marie was right, it *was* good. The work of one of the artists, a woman, particularly appealed to her, and if her finances had been healthier she would have been tempted to buy one or two of the works.

She mentioned this to Peter, and he offered to introduce her to the artist, whom he had met earlier that evening. But looking around he couldn't locate her, and a glance at her watch told Emma that she couldn't stop any longer.

Sean also seemed to have disappeared; at least, she didn't glimpse either him or his blonde as she hurriedly thanked the curator and retrieved her damp umbrella. Perhaps that was just as well, she told herself.

All the same, he must have noticed that she was there. He could have come up and said hello, and he hadn't. She couldn't keep that thought from adding an edge of irritability to her mood as she hurried along the rain-slicked street back to her house.

The first couple of her quilt class pupils had beaten her to it, but Marie, bless her, had made coffee and kept them chatting in the kitchen. Emma wasn't the type to sulk, and genuine gratitude at her friend's thoughtfulness, added to equally genuine enthusiasm for the pictures she had just seen, soon combined to restore her normal cheerful temper.

* * *

It didn't surprise Emma, though it did annoy her, when a knock on her front door early next morning proved to be from Sean.

'Hi, Em,' he announced, as lightly as if it were only five minutes since they'd last spoken. 'Can you spare a few minutes?'

'Not many,' she grudgingly responded.

'I know you're busy—we won't take long.' He gave the door a nudge, since she had barely opened it six inches. 'I was telling Lillie about your quilts, and she's really keen to have a look at them. She's got to get back to London this afternoon, so I wondered if. . .'

Emma had stopped listening. The door, swinging open, had revealed the blonde girl from the gallery, dressed in skin-tight denims and a yellow cotton jumper that was unravelling at the hem.

Anger licked through her. Anger at Sean, rapidly followed by anger at herself, because she knew that she shouldn't be reacting so strongly.

But she was, and it was all she could do to respond with a brusque 'hello', when the blonde girl said a rather uncertain 'hello' to her.

'Just a quick look,' Sean persisted. 'I'll show Lillie if you like, while you get on with your work.'

He'd what? Expect her to keep her stitches even, while he rifled through her things with this blonde bimbo? Some hope she'd have of doing that!

Maybe it didn't justify quite as much annoyance as she actually felt, but she really did think it wasn't on to bring his girlfriend on a sightseeing tour. He knew she didn't like to interrupt her work except for potential clients, and to judge by her jumper Lillie wasn't one of those.

'I'm rather busy,' she said curtly.

'That's good,' Sean said cheerfully. 'I mean, for you—

not for us. Look, if you're pushed I'll help you out a bit. I'm going to Cowes this afternoon; I could leave it till Duncan gets out of school, and take him with me?'

'Thanks,' Emma said, with an effort. She still wished he and his blonde would go away, but common sense told her that wasn't a realistic expectation. Underneath his laid-back manner Sean had a very determined will, and he'd obviously fixed on showing Lillie the quilts. She couldn't make her reluctance any clearer without being downright rude, and she wasn't prepared to do that, so she stepped aside and said brusquely, 'You might as well come in.'

'This is really kind of you,' Lillie said eagerly. 'Sean's told me so much about your quilts, and they sound just the kind of thing I love.'

All right, Emma told herself. It wasn't Lillie's fault that she was five feet nothing and exquisitely pretty. It wasn't Lillie's fault, either, that her boyfriend's blue eyes did strange things to her own insides. She wasn't really all *that* busy, and there wasn't any sensible reason why she shouldn't welcome Lillie's interest.

She took a deep breath, edged as far away from Sean as she could in the narrow hallway, and asked, 'Do you do any quilting yourself?' as she led them through to the kitchen to switch on the kettle, then up the stairs to her workroom.

'I've never tried,' Lillie said apologetically. 'I did do some fabric design at college, but paint's really my medium.'

'As you saw yesterday,' Sean prompted, in a voice that rather implied Emma was being dense.

'I'm sorry, I don't——'

'In the Arts Centre,' Lillie amplified. 'Sean pointed you out to me, but a phone call came through from

London before we could get over to say hello, and when we got out of the office you'd gone.'

Emma stopped dead on the stairs. 'You mean *you're* L. Jane Smithers!'

'I thought you knew. . .'

'Sorry,' Sean said. 'I should have introduced you properly. Lillie Smithers, painter; Emma Morgan, quiltmaker.'

It made a surprising difference. Didn't take away all that treacherous jealousy, needless to say, but there wasn't any way she could feel hostile to the painter whose work she had so admired the evening before.

She stumblingly expressed her approval of Lillie's work, and put out a hand, which Lillie duly shook, before Sean went on, 'Actually you've got Lillie to thank for my moving in next door. She put me on to number nine after she came down to fix up the exhibition.'

'And I did pretty well for you, didn't I, love?' Lillie demanded, beaming at him. She was standing three steps above him, but, since she was so short and Sean so tall, that left their gazes just about level.

While Emma, a step above Lillie and a good six inches taller, didn't figure at all in the exchange. All of a sudden she felt like a spare wheel again, and she turned abruptly to clamber the last few steps to her workroom.

She let loose the sharp edge of her frustration in shaking out a couple of quilts, then spread them across the floor and quilting frame as Lillie and Sean came into the room.

'You'll maybe like these ones best; they're my original designs.'

'Oh, they're glorious!' Lillie exclaimed.

Sean leaned back against the banister post and watched as Lillie and Emma busied themselves with the quilts. It felt to Emma as if his eyes were burning into her back, but she made a point of ignoring him. Which wasn't difficult, since Lillie had an irrepressibly lively personality, and asked even more questions than Sean himself had done.

'Emma,' Sean said, when he could fit a word in edgeways.

'Yes?' She only half turned, without meeting his eyes.

'You haven't shown Lil that sunburst quilt. The cream and red one, you know?'

'Oh—no, I haven't got that any more.'

'You sold it?'

'More or less.' Briefly, she outlined to her two visitors the deal with the Frazers.

'That's nice,' Sean said in a flat voice.

'Sean, don't grump,' Lillie chided. She glanced up at Emma. 'That sounds great,' she said brightly. 'Just what you were looking for, from what Sean told me. He's only sore-headed because you've taken the edge off his news. He's got some plans for you himself.'

'You've what?'

'I'll tell you later,' Sean said offhandedly. Then he seemed to make an effort to overcome his pique, and it was in a more cheerful voice that he went on, 'Hey, how's my quilt going? Have you had a chance to get started on it yet?'

Of course she hadn't, and didn't intend to. But she could hardly say that, so she temporised by saying, 'Not properly, I'm afraid. I've done some planning out, but nothing I can show you yet.'

'You're buying one of these, Sean?'

'Emma's designing one for me.'

'You ought to buy this one.' Lillie eased out of the pile a red and green quilt with a dramatic swirling pattern. 'Imagine that on your brass bed.'

Brass bed! He didn't have a brass bed, Emma thought,

annoyed. She had seen his bedroom when she'd dug out Duncan from his house the day before he'd left, and noticed without pleasure that he slept on a mattress on the floor—which was yet another reason for not taking seriously his commission. And she could do without Lillie hinting that she shared his bed, *thank you*—though perhaps, it belatedly occurred to her, Lillie didn't do so after all, if she wasn't aware of his sleeping arrangements.

'I could buy that too, maybe,' Sean suggested. 'Or you could, Lil.'

'I couldn't afford it right now,' Lillie ruefully responded. 'Maybe if the pictures sell well I'll get one at the end of the exhibition. A couple went at the opening, Emma, but that's all, and my cut for those is barely enough to cover my expenses. And *don't* suggest Emma and I swap a quilt for an oil, Sean, because I couldn't afford that either, and nor could you, could you?'

'Not really, but I'm tempted. I loved one or two of your cityscapes. That market scene. . .'

'That's one of my favourites too,' Sean agreed.

'Cross our fingers, then,' Lillie said. 'If Newport's art lovers go for my paintings, and Ryde's tourists buy a few of your quilts, then. . .'

'We'll see what we can do,' Emma lightly agreed.

Sean might have lingered all morning, but Lillie seemed to appreciate Emma's need to work, and she bustled him away, full of thanks, half an hour later, leaving Emma high on praise, yet still a trifle restless and dissatisfied.

It wasn't really that she envied Lillie for having Sean, she soon decided. Whatever Judy imagined, he wasn't the type of man she wanted for herself. It was just—oh, loneliness and a general kind of longing. When you were alone it sometimes seemed as if the whole world except for you was made up of couples.

So what? They couldn't all be happy couples, any more than she and Neil had been. And didn't she herself have a man in tow? Dave Madison certainly seemed to think so, as he proved shortly afterwards by ringing to invite her out to dinner the following evening.

The invitation didn't thrill her quite as much as Dave seemed to imagine it would, and she temporised, telling him she'd have to find a baby-sitter before she could commit herself. Then she hated herself for weakness and inconsistency and a dozen other inexplicable emotions that chased through her mind before she arrived home after collecting Duncan from school, to find Sean's Peugeot parked on the pavement and Sean himself waiting next to it.

'Work, woman,' he announced, taking her keys from her and unlocking her front door. 'Lots of it—till we call you for supper.'

'You're cooking supper?'

'Would I risk that?' It was a rhetorical question: she already knew he wasn't up to anything more complex than boiled eggs. 'No, we'll pick up a takeaway on the way back from Cowes. Pizza. Any special order?'

'Seafood's my favourite. But Sean, I hadn't meant to corner you into looking after Dunc. Really I was happy to show the quilts to Lillie, and——'

'Now did I say you cornered me? Ask Lil, she'd tell you I'm the original Houdini when it comes to women with cornering on their minds. Coming, Dunc?'

'What're we doing?' Duncan asked eagerly.

'Looking over boats. Can't borrow your mum's dinghy forever—I want to buy my own.'

'It's the wrong season,' Emma couldn't resist saying.

'That's why they're cheap,' Sean flung back at her. 'I want a working design, right? Next-Door Neighbour, then we'll talk terms after supper.'

'Yes, sir,' Emma retorted under her breath as she stumped upstairs, hoping—without much confidence— that Sean could be trusted to make sure Duncan took his wellingtons and parka. Should she go down again and check? No—on second thoughts, he'd think of it. He knew enough about boats and boatyards to realise that waterproof clothes were needed, and he was very reliable with kids, for a man who didn't have any himself. Although she herself hadn't completely forgiven him his earlier defection, Duncan was already acting as if he'd never been gone.

So, to work. Was he serious? Did he *really* want to see working drawings, *and* to pay up a few hundred pounds? It was hard to believe, but there wasn't any other logical explanation for his persistence.

She settled down with squared paper and Schubert, and by the time she was distracted by a clatter downstairs, followed by Duncan's wholesale eruption into her workroom, she had the makings of a sharp but subtle patchwork design of dark triangles chasing each other, overlaid by a quilting pattern of large and small diamonds.

When Duncan dragged her downstairs she found Sean humming to himself as he levered the cork out of a bottle of red wine. He hadn't bothered with a tablecloth, but he had brought down and lit the candles she kept on her shelves, and warmed plates to hold the contents of the shallow mountain of cardboard pizza boxes that, leaning unsteadily, formed the table centrepiece.

'Here's to dinghy races,' he announced, filling two glasses, holding one out to her and raising the other in a semi-ironical toast.

'You've bought one already?'

'I've fixed on a likely one, and agreed I can take it out tomorrow to see how it handles. I told Duncan he could come, unless you've any other plans?'

'That's nice,' Emma said. Duncan had been messing around in boats ever since he had learned to walk, and he was a strong swimmer, so she was happy to trust him with Sean. 'Oh—I half fixed to go out tomorrow evening, so I'll need him back in time to hand over to a baby-sitter. That is, if I can find one.'

'You haven't booked one yet?'

'No, I'll have to phone round this evening.'

'Don't bother. I'll stay with Duncan till you get back.'

'Sean—it's nice of you to offer, but. . .'

'But what?'

Yes, what? But it didn't seem fair to leave Sean to sit with Duncan while she went out with Dave, was what she meant. However, it seemed clear that Sean didn't mind in the slightest. It wasn't as if he was interested in taking her out himself.

'Oh, nothing. Thanks, Sean, I'd be very grateful. I'll do a casserole and leave it in the oven, then the two of you'll be able to eat whenever you get back.'

'Sounds good,' he agreed.

So was the pizza. Sean had brought the seafood she'd ordered, Mexican hot for himself, and ham and mush-room for Duncan. Plus the wine, Coke for Duncan, and a big tub of chocolate ripple ice-cream.

Duncan chomped through his pizza as if he hadn't eaten for a month, devoured two huge portions of ice-cream, then fell asleep on the sofa in the sudden way that only an over-excited child could manage. Emma and Sean drank another glass of wine, and talked in low voices about sailing. Then Sean gently woke Duncan and led him up to bed while Emma cleared away and washed up.

She was still at the sink when he came downstairs, walking up to her from behind and setting his hands on her shoulders.

'Leave the rest,' he said in a low voice.

'No; no, I don't like leaving it. I won't be long. I'll just clear up and make coffee before you go.'

'I wish you'd stop running away from me.'

'I'm not running away.'

'Mentally you are.' His hand flexed her shoulder-joint. 'You've been mad at me all day, and I still don't know why. Feel the tenseness?'

'Stop touching me and I wouldn't *be* tense!'

'I like touching you. You'd like it too, if you'd let yourself.'

'Now why should I want to touch Lillie's boyfriend?'

'Oh,' Sean said, in a voice that told her precisely how vixenish she must have sounded.

'I think that's a perfectly reasonable attitude to take.'

'I don't.' His hands were still on her shoulders, his thumbs on her shoulderblades, working on her taut muscles. 'Anyway, I'm not Lillie's boyfriend. At least, I'm her friend, but I'm not her lover, if that's what you were implying. We went through that and out the other side years ago.'

'Then where were you——?'

'I was in London, that's all. Working.'

'You might have said you were going!'

Sean's hands stilled. There was an uncomfortable moment's silence, then he said slowly, 'I might, true, but I've never been in the habit of telling my friends about my movements.'

'So you think you can just drop in and drop out of our lives when it suits you?'

He thought again, then said, 'To be honest, I never thought of it like that. That's how most of my friends work, but I guess they're a bit different from your friends. I've never lived in a place like Newport before.'

'Down here, we like to know where we are with people.'

'Then I'll warn you before I go next time. OK?'

'OK.'

'So are we friends now?'

She nodded.

'And you'll stop running away?'

'I told you I wasn't.'

'Yes, you were.' He swung her round to face him. 'And not just because you were miffed at me today; you've been doing it all along.'

'You've spent enough time here!'

'True, but doing what? Playing chess with Duncan, playing computer games with Duncan, having supper with you and Duncan. Don't get me wrong, Emma: I like Duncan, he's a great kid, and I'm happy to do things with him. But I don't like it when you always act as if I've come round to see him and not you.'

'I don't!'

'Yes, you do,' he said patiently. 'OK, you need to work, and it's fair enough to nip off and do some sewing while we're playing chess, but every time, when Duncan goes to bed and we've got a chance to relax together, you go and open the front door for me. Even this evening, when you knew as well as I did that we'd got a misunderstanding to sort out once Duncan was out of the way.'

'I didn't do that!'

'So why the coffee in such a rush, "before I go"? It's not nine o'clock yet. It might be little boys' bedtime, but it's not my bedtime, or yours. Do you really want me to go now? Aren't I allowed to stay till the end of the evening?'

'Well. . .yes, of course, if you want to.'

'Actually I was hoping to. There's a play on television

I want to watch. I bought myself a set yesterday but they won't be delivering it till Monday, so I haven't got one next door.'

'Then watch it here. Sure, of course, I don't mind.'

'And you'll join me?'

'Obviously. I don't mind watching the telly.'

'Such enthusiasm.' His hands, still on her shoulders, tightened their grip slightly. Then he slid them down her arms, in a smooth easy movement, and on to the curve of her hips.

In spite of herself, a tremor went through her.

'Em, you're not afraid of me?'

Of course she was! She was afraid of meeting the searching look in his blue eyes. She was afraid of the effect his touch was having on her. She was afraid, most of all, of the urge that gripped her, to lean backwards and let her body collide with the tall solid mass of his.

'I. . . I'm not. . .'

'This isn't meant as a pass,' Sean said softly. 'I just want us to be friends.'

'We are.'

'Good. Then I'll help you finish the washing-up and make coffee, and we'll go and watch the programme together.'

It seemed such a reasonable suggestion that she couldn't think how to object to it—and, although she still felt a little uneasy, in a way she didn't want to object. It was ridiculous of her to be so conscious of him that she took every casual touch as a threat. His caress hadn't been overtly sexual, and they were surely neither of them so out of control that a simple hug would lead inevitably to more. Out of practice with men she admitted to being, but she didn't want to become the sort of freak who jumped every time somebody touched her.

So, with an effort, she matched his casual chat as they

cleared up in the kitchen, then followed him through to
the living-room. She made for an armchair near the
window, but he caught her hand, and drew her down
instead on to the sofa next to him.

It would have been equally ridiculous to object when
he slipped his arm across her shoulders, and guided her
head down to nestle in the angle between his arm and
torso. His hand stroked the fall of her chestnut hair and
the curve of her far shoulder, in a slow, lazy, rhythmic
motion that eased her towards relaxation, and as the
minutes slipped by and he made no effort to take his
caresses any further she found the tension leaching out
of her.

In fact it was nice curling up with him; very nice. She
slipped off her shoes and tucked her feet up under her
thighs, and didn't let herself mind when the movement
tipped her off balance, and left her leaning more heavily
against him. It was a while since she'd cuddled up with
anyone other than Duncan, and she had missed the
simple pleasure of it.

The television play was good, too. It was a whodunnit,
but an amusing one, featuring a way-out detective called
Silas South and his basset hound Thumper. Although
she was weary, Emma soon became absorbed in the
intricate plot—and predictably annoyed when her guess
at the murderer turned out to be wrong.

'Didn't *you* think it was Macmillan?' she demanded,
as Sean uncurled himself and crossed over to switch off
the set. 'I could have sworn it was going to be.'

'That was the idea.'

'But there weren't *any* clues pointing to Mrs Graham.'

'Yes, there were,' was Sean's cool riposte. 'You saw
her hiding her gloves in the sewing-box in that scene at
the start, and then when she went to the bottom of the
garden——'

'Oh, you know-it-all!'

'I could hardly fail to, could I?'

'But did you really——'

'Emma,' he said, shaking his head and wearing an odd half-smile, 'you weren't paying attention.'

'All right, you don't have to tell me I'm being dense. I'm tired.'

'Paying attention to the credits, to be precise.' Seeing her blank expression, he amplified, 'The writer, for instance?'

'The. . . Sean, you didn't!' she exclaimed, jerking upright on the sofa.

'I thought you knew—Silas South's my mainstay,' he told her cheerfully, reclaiming his seat. 'Come to that, it's the TV adaptation that's paying for number nine.'

'But that's marvellous!' she exclaimed, before her admiration was overlaid by guilt. She had a strong suspicion he'd mentioned Silas South before, and she hadn't troubled to remember the name. Nor had she thought to look for his books in bookshops; she had just taken it for granted that they wouldn't be there.

'I should have known,' she apologised awkwardly. 'I mean, you said you wrote detective stories, but——'

'But you didn't think I was good enough to get them on the telly?' He grinned, and squeezed her shoulders. 'Nor did I, for ages! That's the first one I've ever had on. But they're talking about doing a Silas South series if this pilot's well reviewed, so. . .'

'You mean you've written lots?'

'Eleven novels, so far. More coffee?'

'You dark horse,' Emma marvelled.

But she knew he hadn't been, if she was honest. He'd told her nothing but the truth: it was she who had prejudged him, reading the wrong things between the lines.

Even now, she found it hard to believe. Eleven novels! All right, a word processor and several shelves full of books figured among the scanty furnishings of number nine, but she'd still taken his working life to be a pretty casual affair. That wasn't only because she compared him with Neil; he genuinely did have a laid-back approach to life, and even now that she knew it was hard to imagine him buckling down to anything resembling hard work.

Eleven novels didn't write themselves, though.

'Yes, coffee,' Sean answered himself, getting up and going to make it.

Emma sat in the dim light considering for a while. Then she got up too, and she padded through to the kitchen in her bare feet.

She trailed to a halt when she'd got through the door. Sean was leaning against the far counter, facing towards her, his hands stuck deep in the pockets of his cord trousers.

He'd heard her coming, as she knew from the way his blue eyes were fixed steadily on her, but he didn't approach; just stood there, letting her gaze at him. Which she did, her self-consciousness overtaken for once by the sheer need to re-evaluate what she made of him.

Drifter, drop-out: that was what his appearance had spelled to her. No wonder, really—with hair that was a little shorter but no less dishevelled than when she'd first met him, a disreputable navy blue sweatshirt advertising a two-year-old folk festival, and the red trainers that seemed to be his only shoes, he certainly wasn't a power dresser.

Artistic-casual didn't necessarily equate with failure, though; not being interested in clothes wasn't the same as not being able to afford new ones. Eccentric writer fitted the evidence just as well.

Her feeling of awkwardness came roaring back then, with redoubled force, because she knew she had just demolished one of the defences she had set up against caring too much for him. She hated herself for having been over-influenced by appearances; hated herself even more for wanting him more, now that she knew he wasn't the kind of failure Neil had been.

Except that she had wanted him all along, and known it, and been fighting it.

'Happy now?' Sean asked in a lightly amused voice.

'Confused, mainly.'

'I'm not a superstar, you know. Not a millionaire.'

'I know,' she retorted. 'Sorry. Did you make the coffee?'

'Kettle's boiled. I'll make it in a minute.' Instead he pushed himself off the counter and prowled across the room towards her.

'I'll have to read your books,' Emma gabbled, panicking. 'I mean, I liked the programme, I really did, and. . .'

'Doesn't matter.' He reached out his hands to her, first slowly, then turning the movement into a sudden grab, catching her hands as if he was expecting her to run away.

Which she might have done, if her legs would have carried her.

'Emma, you can't still be scared of me,' he said aggrievedly.

'No, I'm scared of me,' she flung back; then turned her head away, appalled at herself.

A frown skittered across Sean's face; but he showed no sign of having taken it into account as he carried her hands, still trapped in his, round to the small of her back. The movement brought her body hard up against his, pressing her to him; and she felt him catch his breath exultantly.

He wasn't relaxed any more. The suppressed power in his arms, holding her trapped, seemed to feed through into the rest of his body: into the tensed muscles of his chest and shoulders, into the shallow rasp of his now resumed breathing, into the growing hardness that she felt against her lower body. Friendship wasn't the word for this; sexual awareness filled the small room.

Sean bent his head and touched his lips to her hair. Then to her cheekbone; then, still holding her hands behind her back, he nudged her head upwards and claimed her lips with his own.

At five feet six she wasn't short, but he was a good head taller, and her bare feet didn't do anything to ease her vulnerability. He seemed to surround and enfold her. His mouth tasted of wine and chilli and, indefinably, of man. But in spite of the air of expectation that surrounded them his kiss was exploratory rather than demanding, the pressure of his lips confident but light.

'Mmm,' he murmured, drawing them away from hers. 'You ought to be kissed more often.'

'I don't think I——'

'There's such a thing,' Sean responded, dropping a trail of chilli-hot kisses across her forehead and down to her ear, 'as thinking too much.'

'You said you wouldn't make a pass at me.'

'This isn't a pass,' Sean replied reasonably. 'It's only a kiss.'

His lips, finding hers again, didn't feel like *only* anything. Invisible electric circuits carried the charged effect from her mouth to the breasts that seemed to swell beneath her tight sweater, to her fingertips, her loins. Sean's fingers followed, cupping one wool-covered

breast, then easing her sweater up at the waist and
sneaking a hand beneath it.

She gasped as his thumb found and teased a nipple,
inadequately protected by a film of lace. A flick, a rolling
caress, and it had hardened into a sharp point of pure
sensation.

Her lips parted in a sigh of excitement, and as Sean's
hand moved, tracing out the full lower curve of her
breast, his tongue nudged her teeth apart and thrust
forward to find hers.

Her nipple ached for more of his touch, but his elusive
fingers marched in a teasing circle around it. His tongue
paused only to greet hers, fence for an instant, then
withdraw. He lowered his head, and licked a trail of
sensation around the high round neck of her sweater.

His tongue, his lips, his hands, were moving with all
the tantalising restlessness that was quintessentially
Sean: touching and teasing, then drifting on almost
before she could absorb each sensation enough to
respond to it. Emma brought one of her newly freed
hands up to his shoulders, and groped for the leverage
to hug herself more tightly to him; but she hadn't caught
firm grip on the smooth jersey before he moved yet
again, this time taking hold of her upper arms and easing
her away from him.

'Just——' he bent down and dropped the lightest of
kisses on the end of her nose '—a kiss.'

Her rapid breathing eased, and her eyes slowly re-
focused on him as he moved, in a lazy lope, back to the
steaming kettle.

Damn him. Damn that elusive quality in him, that
had him whistling as he spooned the coffee into the
cafetière, while she was about ready to scream with the
intensity of unassuaged longing.

Just a kiss. Maybe, to him, that was all it had been.

But he had been aroused too, she thought silently. She had had unmistakable evidence of that. If this was Sean's idea of a platonic friendship, then perhaps she wasn't the only one who had been kidding herself. There was something a little *too* determinedly light-hearted about his movements now, as if he was making a performance out of his indifference. If he *hadn't* kept his caresses brief and elusive, then perhaps. . .

'I haven't told you yet,' Sean said, 'about my plans for you and your quilts.'

'Tell me some other time.'

The sharpness in her voice made him turn to her. He held her eyes for an instant, then raised his eyebrows, in a slightly theatrical 'what now?' gesture.

'It was only a kiss,' he said. 'A very nice kiss. Wasn't it?'

Yes—and no, she thought to herself.

She shrugged. 'I suppose so.'

'Haven't you kissed anyone else since your husband died?'

'Once or twice.'

'Well, then.' He turned back to the counter, found a tablespoon, gave the coffee a good stir and put back the lid and plunger. 'Friends?'

'Yes, but. . . Don't do that again, Sean.'

'I'm sorry. I thought you wanted it too.' He didn't sound upset; a little intrigued perhaps, uncomprehending—rather too uncomprehending, because she'd already had evidence that evening that he was a good psychologist, and she couldn't really believe that he didn't understand her feelings. 'Want it black?' he went on, his voice supremely casual.

And what option did she have but to put on a casual tone of her own, and say lightly, as if she'd forgotten the incident already, 'Actually I hate black coffee. I'll have it white with half a sugar, please.'?

CHAPTER FIVE

'DRINK and biscuit time. Oh, you've beaten us to it,' Sean remarked, shepherding Duncan before him into Emma's kitchen, and finding her sitting at the table with a coffee-mug and that morning's edition of the *Newport Herald* spread out in front of her.

'Kettle's still warm,' she assured him, and rose to see to the two of them.

She hadn't intended Duncan to spend the morning with Sean, not when he'd already promised to take Dunc for the afternoon and evening, but her son had rushed next door an hour earlier with barely a shouted goodbye to her, and this was the first time she had seen him since.

'Pass the biscuits, that's a good lad,' Sean said, grabbing a chair and swivelling the paper round so that he could see what she had been reading. 'Oho! You're a secret horoscope freak.'

'Not that secret,' Emma retorted. 'It's my friend Judy who writes them. I always read her forecasts and she's done a few proper readings for me too.'

'I'll have to meet her,' Sean said absently, eyes on the paper. 'I never believe horoscopes, but I'm a great fan of astrologers.'

'Now that's a contradiction, if ever there was one.'

'Not really. It's my Gemini dual personality coming out.'

'Oh, and I had you down for an Aquarian.'

'Why's that?'

'Judy's verdict, actually, from what she'd heard of

81

you—not from me, particularly. Imaginative and unpredictable, that's Aquarius.'

'"Water-bearer you may be,"' Sean read out loud, '"but remember you're an air sign at heart. Today could bring a boat trip, so be careful to keep your feet dry." Actually I prefer the Gemini forecast: that goes on about Venus in the fifth house leading to romantic entanglements. Judy's right, of course. I've got the Moon in Gemini, but my Sun's in Aquarius, with Leo rising.'

'You know all about it.'

'I told you, I like astrologers.' He glanced up, his eyes alight with amusement. 'I wasn't kidding you. I haven't much time for fortune-telling: I'd rather believe in free will. But I've known quite a few astrologers, my sister included, and been fond of them all.'

'You'd like Judy.'

'Nice job for you—introduce me. Which is your sign?'

'Taurus. Reliable and plodding, but redeemed from being totally boring by *my* Leo rising.'

'It's a good night for wining and dining, then. Is that what you're planning?'

'Yes, it is, actually.'

'Clever Judy. Mind you, it's a pretty reliable bet for a Saturday night.'

'As are boat trips, for readers who live on a small island.'

'True; but she's got that right as well, hasn't she, Dunc? Clever lady, your friend.'

'Intuitive's the word, I'd say.'

'That's what most of it comes down to.' Sean reached lazily into the biscuit tin and began to munch a Jaffa cake. 'Mmm,' he murmured, 'you bought my favourites.'

'Sheer coincidence,' Emma retorted, not very accurately.

'Sean,' Duncan asked, 'will you come and play Dandy on my computer?'

'You do it, kid. I want to tell your mother about my grand plans for her.'

Emma endorsed this verdict, hovered until she had ensured that Duncan had the computer game loaded successfully, then returned to sit opposite Sean.

She wasn't expecting much from the 'plans' that Lillie had mentioned the day before, but it soon became apparent that once more she had underestimated Sean. He had clearly put a great deal of effort into thinking how he might help her develop her career, and he had come up with two promising suggestions.

One was fairly predictable, though none the less welcome for that. It appeared that one of his many friends ran a prestigious craft shop in Chelsea, and Sean had sounded her out to see if she would be interested in displaying Emma's work. Though Celia wouldn't give a firm commitment without seeing the quilts, she had expressed a lot of interest, and Sean was confident that she would agree to take some work, and would ensure that Emma got a top price for it.

His other suggestion Emma was less sure about. Yet another couple of friends ran a luxury hotel on the Island itself, near Shanklin. They had recently started running a series of winter 'interest weekends', laying on cookery courses, courses in Roman history and so on for guests, and Sean had suggested that Emma might act as tutor on a quilting weekend.

'Don't you think that sounds great?' Sean enthused. 'You'll spend the weekend at the Prince Regent, which is a lovely hotel with a swimming-pool and tennis courts and the kind of food you'll drool over. You'll be paid—not a fortune, but enough—to run the course, and you'll have a chance to sell your quilts to the guests. It's an expensive hotel, so they're the sort of people who've got money to burn.'

'That part sounds good, Sean, but didn't it strike you it's simply not practicable?'

'No, it didn't.'

'Well, it isn't.'

'And why's that?'

'Because of Duncan!' Emma retorted, more than a little exasperated at his short-sightedness. 'If I were on my own I'd leap at the chance, but I'm not. I'm a single parent, and I couldn't leave Dunc for a whole weekend, however much money they offered me.'

'Take him with you.'

'To a posh hotel? He'd hate it. Anyway he needs my attention, and if I was busy teaching people quilting I wouldn't be able to have it, would he?'

'You wouldn't teach all day,' Sean objected. 'Duncan's not a baby. He could amuse himself while you worked, especially in a place like that where there's loads to do. I'd help too.'

'I couldn't ask you to give up your weekend so that I could teach quilting.'

'You didn't have to ask: I offered. I'd like to see more of Bob and Anna, and they've told me I'm welcome to a room any time they've space to spare. And while the weather's good I could use a crew for my boat, assuming the tryout goes OK this afternoon, so. . .'

'What it comes to is, you're determined to make me do it.'

'Em, I didn't think it'd be a question of *making you*,' Sean protested. 'I thought you needed some contacts, and I was helping you by lining them up.'

'I did, and you have helped, and thank you.' She reached out, a little tentatively, and took his hand. 'I'm sorry if I sound grumpy. Blame my Taurean resistance to change! It's just—well, partly that I'm the sort who likes to check whether the ground's solid before I rush into things, and partly that the offer's come at the wrong time.'

'These Frazer people aren't going to sell *all* your work, are they?'

'Most of it. They were talking of taking forty quilts a year.'

'And you've promised them you'll supply that many?'

'More or less.'

'How much more or less? What does your agreement say?'

'It isn't a written agreement, just an understanding— and OK, it might not work out as that many. But I've promised them now, Sean, and I don't feel I could go back on that, even if your friends did make me a better offer.'

'I wasn't suggesting you should,' Sean assured her. But he *was* determined to have her follow up his contacts, and he persisted, probing into the details of her agreement with the Frazers, and making some rather scathing remarks about its vagueness. *His* friend, he pointed out, had provided a written copy of her terms, to be signed by both her and Emma before any work was handed over.

Emma wasn't pleased by this criticism, but she had to admit that he had a point. She hadn't seen the Frazers' shop yet, and didn't even know precisely when it was to open. Perhaps it would be as well, she reluctantly agreed, if she didn't deliver them any more quilts until she had made sure the arrangement was working well.

As Sean pointed out, this would enable her to offer a couple of quilts to his London friend, and she suggested that he come upstairs and choose suitable ones. He was planning to return to London the following week, so he would be able to take them with him then.

'And I want you to agree to try just one weekend at the Prince Regent,' he continued. 'We'll make sure it's one I can make too, so I can help with Duncan. If that really will leave you pushed for time, you can postpone doing the quilt for me.'

'Oh, no, I was going to start on that this afternoon,' Emma assured him. They haggled in a friendly fashion over the price for his quilt, then, after a check that Duncan was still absorbed in his game, they retreated upstairs to sort through the depleted pile, and choose two beautiful hand-sewn quilts for Sean to take to London.

Sean was friendly this morning, but even when the two of them were alone he was wary, as if the incident the night before had taken things further than he, too, wanted them to go. He didn't touch her again, and Emma began slowly to think that maybe she might be able to enjoy a platonic friendship with him after all.

It was a good day. Though it was October the sun shone brightly, and the brisk breeze was an advantage from Sean's and Duncan's viewpoint. The three of them ate a light lunch of home-made vegetable soup, then the two sailors set off, and Emma was left to whizz through the housework then retreat upstairs to her workroom.

She made a good start on the Next-Door Neighbour quilt, selecting and cutting the fabrics and sorting them ready for sewing. By seven there was still no sign of Sean and Duncan—not that she had expected them back early on such a lovely day—so she showered and changed in the strangely silent house, then switched on the radio to cheer herself up while she fixed her hair and completed her make-up.

Sean knew she was going out to dinner with another man, so there wasn't any reason to feel guilty about her plans, but still they made her a little uneasy. Trouble was, she thought uncomfortably, that kiss the night before had made too much impression on her for comfort.

Sean himself made too much impression. She felt reasonably confident that he really wasn't looking for an affair, any more than she was; but it didn't seem right that her mind should be on him all the time she was preparing for a date with another man.

Exploring possibilities with Dave had seemed like such a good idea: it was time she got over the trauma of Neil's death, and set about rebuilding her life. But was that really what she was doing? Wasn't it more the case that she was making use of Dave to counterbalance her attraction to Sean?

Dave obviously had needs and feelings too, and she didn't want to be unfair to him. What was more, she guessed that while Sean was unconventional enough not to turn a hair at the prospect of baby-sitting while she went out with another man, Dave might not appreciate her domestic arrangements in the slightest.

It was all too easy to envisage a series of embarrassing scenes developing. If Dave came in when he called round to pick her up, or if he came back for coffee after their date, there would be one man too many around—and it might not be Sean who found himself playing gooseberry!

But it was too late to change the arrangements now; and if she couldn't help wondering how Sean would react when he saw her in her peach jersey dress, which had a flatteringly low wrapover neckline and short skirt, then at least Dave wasn't to know that.

As it happened, Sean and Duncan still hadn't returned

when Dave appeared at eight o'clock. He had brought her flowers, a big bunch of asters, and was looking extremely smart in a well-cut dark suit.

Dave had booked a table for them at Valentino's, one of the swishest restaurants in the area. It was months since Emma had been out to a restaurant for dinner, and although she wasn't enthralled at the way he ordered without consulting her she thoroughly enjoyed the excellent Italian cuisine.

When she had seen Dave since the break-up of his marriage it had been with Ben and Duncan in tow, and preparing for the date she had found herself wondering what they would find to talk about when the children weren't there to distract them. He worked as a dentist, which was admirable in its way, but not a subject she relished over dinner. But he was also a governor of the local school Ben and Duncan attended, and active in the local Rotary Club, she discovered. They chatted about carnival committees and fund-raising dinners, school curricula and mutual friends, all of which kept them going happily until the waiter cleared away their dessert plates and suggested coffee.

'I thought we might skip the coffee here, and I'll beg some off you when I get you home?' Dave suggested. 'You've a baby-sitter, haven't you, so you won't want to be too late back?'

Emma bit her lip. 'That's thoughtful of you, Dave, but actually I've got a neighbour sitting tonight, so it shouldn't be a problem.'

'You'd like coffee here, then?' To her relief he didn't argue, but ordered two—and offered her a brandy, which she declined since he was driving and wouldn't be able to join her.

'So who's the neighbour?' he asked, as the waiter moved away.

'Sean Davies,' Emma said, and went on to tell him about Sean's work as a writer, and to mention the Silas South programme, which Dave too proved to have watched and enjoyed.

'Seems a strange way for a man to spend Saturday night,' was his only other comment, to which she didn't respond. She suspected he had forgotten his brief encounter with Sean in the Wheatsheaf, and instead formed the impression that her neighbour was either reclusive or old and doddery. It didn't seem the moment to put him right.

After two cups of coffee in the restaurant it wasn't difficult to keep Dave from coming in when he dropped her back at number seven, although the lingering kiss he gave her in his car suggested he wouldn't have minded an invitation. 'I'll see you soon,' he murmured in a husky voice, and Emma, relieved that the evening had gone so well, was happy to agree with him.

He *was* a nice man. Not thrilling, but nice. All right, he had seemed just a tiny bit boring after Sean, but then that was true of almost everybody, compared to Sean. At least he was stable and reliable, and perhaps with time she'd acquire warmer feelings for him. It was certainly worth trying, when there wasn't another suitable man in the picture.

Only the unstable, unreliable, generally unsuitable one she was just returning to. She paused in the hallway, armouring herself by dwelling on Dave's kiss. OK, it hadn't set her on fire, but it had been a nice kiss. A genuine, uncomplicatedly nice kiss, unlike. . .

Enough of that. Where *was* Sean, anyway? She couldn't hear the television or the stereo, and he hadn't responded to her slamming the front door. He was *there*, wasn't he? He wouldn't have left Duncan alone. . .?

No, he hadn't left Duncan alone. He was in the living-room. He'd pulled a low table across in front of the sofa, and was hunched over the portable word processor he'd brought across from number nine.

'You're working?'

'Oh!' He jumped, as if he hadn't taken in the clicks and rustles of her arrival. Then grinned apologetically, pushing his hair back from his forehead with a restless hand, and said, 'Sorry. I'm in mid-scene, so make some coffee, there's a love, and leave me to it.'

Leave him to it! At ten past eleven in her living-room! Shaking her head, Emma withdrew to the kitchen.

There wasn't another peep out of Sean as she brewed the coffee, and even the loud rattle as she deposited his mug by the screen didn't provoke more than an abstracted 'Thanks'. Emma took her own mug and claimed the chair opposite.

He was still in his sailing clothes, bar the jacket he'd thrown over the back of the sofa, and the only glass within range looked to be half full of water. For a few minutes she watched, fascinated by his absorption and yet rather hoping that he would be distracted enough by her to abandon it—which he wasn't. Then she went upstairs to check on Duncan. His clothes were strewn across his bedroom floor, but he was at least in his clean pyjamas and smelling satisfactorily of toothpaste.

'Excuse me interrupting,' she said as mildly as she could manage half an hour later—and a long half-hour it had seemed too, with the silence broken by nothing but the click of the computer keyboard and Sean's occasional low curse—'but could you tell me how long you plan to take?'

'Uh? Oh, no idea. Go to bed if you want. I'll let myself out.'

'You wouldn't like some more coffee?' Silly question really, when he hadn't touched his original mugful.

'No, thanks.' This time he did at least look up. 'You don't mind, do you? If I move the computer next door I'll lose my train of thought.'

'Oh no, do stay.'

That hardly needed saying, since he clearly hadn't any intention of doing anything else. It wasn't as if she could complain, when he had been such a help to her and Duncan all day, but still it grated to go upstairs and undress leaving him to work away in semi-darkness below her.

She leaned her head over the banisters when she was in her nightdress, and listened out. She could just hear his faint tap-tap, and it was past midnight now. Shaking her head, she retreated to her bedroom, and after a restless ten minutes or so she fell into a smooth and dreamless sleep.

It wasn't really a surprise when Duncan woke her next morning, announcing in an excited voice that Sean was asleep on the sofa downstairs.

'Is he, love?' Emma asked wearily, checking her watch and discovering that it was seven-forty. 'Look, he must be tired, and so am I, so go and play in your bedroom for a while, OK?'

'What time shall I wake you up again?'

'Nine,' she murmured, turning her head back to the pillow and barely hearing him leave.

But she wasn't a late sleeper, and habit made her resurface at eight-fifteen. She and Duncan crept around washing and dressing, then at a quarter to nine they ventured cautiously downstairs and switched on the kettle.

Emma sneaked into the living-room, and had to

suppress a smile at the sight that greeted her. Sean was sprawled out on his back, still fully dressed apart from his trainers—which sat on the floor beside him—with a heap of cushions piled beneath his head. The sofa was a three-seater, but it still wasn't quite long enough to accommodate his long body, and his feet, clad in holey yellow socks, dangled over the near end.

He had at least remembered to switch off the word processor.

She coughed.

Sean's right eye opened, and gave her a watery look. He closed it again, then a moment later he opened both eyes and focused on her more convincingly.

'Morning,' Emma said brightly. 'Like a cup of tea? Toast? Orange juice?'

'Mmm. Orange juice, please. Big glass.'

'One orange juice coming up.'

By the time she had poured it, he had joined her in the kitchen. 'Great service here,' he announced, taking the glass out of her hands and downing all its contents.

'Sean, would it be rude to ask what time you went to sleep last night?'

'Couldn't tell you exactly—maybe fourish.'

'I hope you finished your scene all right.'

'Finished the chapter. Good night's work that was. You'll have to read it.' He grinned disarmingly.

'That's nice.'

'Em, what makes me think you're mad at me?'

'I'm not mad *at* you,' Emma corrected, very precisely. 'I just think you *are* mad.'

'I like working at night: no distractions.'

'You don't feel a little—er—washed out in the morning?'

'Not generally. Did I hear you mention breakfast? Maybe I should go home and wash first.'

'Maybe you should.'

He put down the orange-juice glass, leaned forward, and deposited a kiss on her forehead. Then chucked her under the chin, turned to grin at Duncan, and ambled towards the front door.

'Mum,' Duncan said, as soon as he'd gone, 'can I work at night when I'm grown up?'

It was lucky for Sean, Emma reluctantly conceded, that he seemed to be the sort of person who didn't need much sleep. After breakfast he was as energetic as ever. He hauled Duncan down to the football fields, from whence they returned extremely muddy at lunchtime, cajoled Emma into stretching her roast lamb to feed him too, and filled her in with all the details of his new boat—the trip the day before had been a great success, and the deal was now signed—over lunch.

After lunch he talked Emma and Duncan into showing him around Carisbrooke Castle, a ruined medieval fortress not far from Newport. Though Emma had taken Duncan there before, it was two years or more since their last visit—long enough to make everything seem fresh to a nine-year-old.

Sean might have been nine too, she thought, amused, as she watched him and Duncan scrambling up and down steep banks and ditches, throwing pennies down the well in the keep, and marvelling at the second well, where water was drawn up by a treadwheel driven by a donkey.

She would have been happy to stand and watch all afternoon while the two of them cavorted, but after half an hour Sean sent Duncan off to explore the barbican on his own, and joined her on the ramparts.

And there it was again: that raw tension between them, which couldn't be all on her side, surely.

'Lovely day again,' Sean remarked, rather unnecessarily.

'Lovely weekend.' She looked away from him, out over the expanse of yellow stone, the green lawns with Duncan's tiny figure receding into the distance, the rolling hills beyond, and with a sudden desire to goad him added, 'You haven't asked me about last night.'

'So I haven't.'

'Don't you want to know?'

'I can't say I do.'

'You haven't even asked who I went out with.'

'Dave somebody—Duncan told me.'

'And you're happy just to leave it at that?'

'Emma, what do you expect?' His voice had risen a little, and there was a ragged edge of annoyance in it. 'It's none of my business who you go out with on Saturday nights. Am I supposed to give you the third degree when you get home?'

'You're my friend, or so you said. Usually my friends are interested in who I see and what I do.'

Silence. She had shaken him a little, she thought with satisfaction; caught him in an inconsistency.

But his voice was restored to its usual light, calm pitch when he finally said, 'That's one point of view, but it's not one I subscribe to. I'm a great believer in freedom and privacy. Curiosity taken too far tends to kill privacy. I don't own my friends, and I don't think I've the right to know all about their lives. What they do is their business, except when it touches me.'

'And this doesn't touch you?' Emma persisted, a little unwisely.

'If you're expecting me to turn green for the sake of your ego,' Sean retorted, 'then you're out of luck.'

Having said which, he half ran, half vaulted down the

nearest stone staircase, and loped across the courtyard towards the barbican and Duncan.

Emma stood on the ramparts, watching as the two of them joined up, just beyond the gate at the far end of the courtyard—and fighting a surge of sheer anger, half with herself and half with Sean.

What was it about him that made her always want more? A touch, a kiss, a smile wasn't enough, not when he'd promptly slither away and turn his attention to something or somebody else. She wanted to *keep* him. Freedom and privacy were all very well, but there were times when they struck her as synonyms for loneliness. What about intimacy, closeness, trust? Didn't Sean share her longing for those things?

What she wanted, she thought ruefully, was for him to be as jealous of Dave as she had been of Lillie—only he wasn't. Maybe his Aquarian nature really was so different from hers that he didn't feel jealousy at all. Even if he did suffer from the odd twinge, he clearly wasn't inclined to admit it.

The knowledge that she'd riled him a little might have provided her with some satisfaction, but it only seemed to point up the gulf between them. When she rejoined him and Duncan there was a coolly distancing edge to his friendliness, and as soon as they got back home he announced that he ought to do some more work, and disappeared into number nine.

Sean working on a book turned out to be quite different from Sean in between books. His Saturday evening absorption in Silas South's case was the rule, not the exception, as Emma soon discovered. His trip to London was over—and the quilts delivered—in a single day, and for the next couple of weeks he worked continually on the book.

And did he work! When he was caught up in his writing he'd forget to wash, forget to eat, forget to go to bed.

Forget to answer the doorbell too, until Emma caught him in the street a couple of mornings later, and persuaded him to give her a key. After that she sent Duncan round to number nine just before suppertime each evening, with orders to force Sean to surface.

Which he did, good-naturedly on the whole, showering and changing before coming round, and always making a contribution to the supper she offered him, bringing a bottle of wine, or a bunch of grapes, or once telling her to leave supper to him the following day, and fetching an Indian takeaway. He'd linger for an hour or so after supper, playing chess with Duncan or watching the early evening television, then he'd go back home to work some more, and she would do the same.

Romance didn't come into the equation, and entire evenings spent relaxing were out of the question while he was writing at full throttle. He clearly hadn't the energy to spare for any more serious attempts to deepen their friendship, and Emma told herself that was all for the best.

She was working hard, too. The Arabic-pattern quilt, a heap of cushions, projects for her quilting classes, and the Next-Door Neighbour quilt filled her workroom and her days. Dave rang a couple of times, and once she went to the cinema with him, but he too seemed to have hit a busy patch, and Emma wasn't sorry to let things drift a little.

Until Sean came round unbidden on the Wednesday ten days after their afternoon at Carisbrooke—and at five, not six—and thrust an untidy heap of typescript into her hands, with the injunction, 'Read that. Please.'

'You've finished it?'

'First draft; it still needs polishing up, but I always like to get people to read it through at this stage, to make sure the plot's clear. If you don't mind? I'll get fish and chips for supper.'

People. That was nice, being just one of the 'people' he was asking. She wanted—too much as usual, she thought ruefully. After all, she *was* only one of Sean's many friends; and, since she valued his friendship, she could hardly refuse this request. She curled up in the armchair by the window while he joined Duncan at the computer, and began to read.

When haddock and chips were placed in front of her she was still reading. She put the book down so that she could give her attention to Duncan for a while before his bedtime, then picked it up again once he was in bed, while Sean made coffee, played a couple of her records at low volume, did the cryptic crossword in the *Herald*.

Fortunately she was a speedy reader, and just before eleven o'clock she set the last page of typescript on the pile by her chair, and announced, 'Yes.'

'Yes what? Is it OK?'

'I like it: it's lively and entertaining, surprisingly like hearing you talk. But there are one or two passages where I wasn't. . .'

They weren't real criticisms she made so much as comments on points which she thought needed clarification. She had read the text closely, sensing that she'd have to work at it if she wanted to earn a permanent place among the people he asked to read his work. From his response she sensed—with satisfaction—that he was pleased by her comments, not simply because they were approving, but because she had made a real effort to help him.

'That's great,' he said. 'I half knew I'd made a mess

of that graveyard scene, but I couldn't see before now
how to put it right. I'll definitely ask you to do this
again!'

'I enjoyed it,' Emma assured him.

'That's hard to believe, but I'm grateful anyway.' He
crossed over to where she sat, collected up the heap of
typed pages from the floor, then dumped them on the
coffee-table and reached out his hands to her.

She let him pull her to her feet; and it wasn't a
conscious decision, merely a natural progression, that
brought her into his arms. He wrapped them around her
and held her in a tight hug; not moving to kiss her,
simply showing his affection.

Except that things were rarely that simple between a
man and a woman—especially when the man was Sean,
and the effect he had on her seemed to deepen all the
time in its intensity. She couldn't hold him like that
without feeling her body surge into life and clamour for
more. And perhaps he felt the same way, because he
rapidly eased out of the embrace, saying a little awkwardly, 'I owe you dinner for that.'

'Of course you don't,' she retorted, inexplicably
crossly.

'All right, I don't, but all the same I'd like to take you
out to dinner one evening. Wouldn't you like that?'

'Well. . .yes, but it wouldn't do, Sean. I'm going out
with Dave, and he wouldn't be pleased if——'

'Don't be ridiculous,' Sean said brusquely. 'Dave
doesn't own you, does he?'

'For dinners out he does. Seriously, Sean. Maybe in
your exotic bohemian circles it's OK to take a different
girl out every night, but it's not the norm in Newport.
Unless you want me to stop seeing Dave, and——'

'No, of course not.'

'*Of course not*?' she echoed bleakly.

'Why should you? I wasn't bidding to be the only man

you ever went out to dinner with, I was just suggesting a
night out before I went back to London.'

'You're going back to London?'

'For a while: I've got to show my editor this draft,
then there must be a mountain of things piling up for me
to do there. I'll be back,' he added, more conciliatorily,
sensing her rigidity. 'But obviously you'd be stupid to
throw up Dave. I don't want to come between you and
him.'

'I see.'

Of course she saw, she thought to herself, exasperated,
as soon as she had said that. It was stupid of her to make
her disappointment so evident. Sean had made it clear
from the start that he wasn't looking for anything more
than an uncommitted friendship. Except that, over the
days and weeks, she had somehow begun to think. . .

But she had certainly been wrong there. Obviously
Sean's lack of jealousy towards Dave was perfectly
genuine, and he wasn't interested in offering her a future
himself. Really she ought to be discouraging him from
coming around so often when he *was* in Newport, and
working on developing her rather stagnant relationship
with Dave instead.

'If you're going soon,' she announced, turning her
back on him and wandering over towards the uncur-
tained windows that gave out on to the river, 'I'll have
to pull my finger out and finish your quilt. There's only
a little more to do, but I'd been letting it ride while I
finish some other jobs.'

'I'll go on Saturday, I thought. Could you finish the
quilt by Friday?'

She nodded.

'Then bring it round Friday afternoon. And—look,
that would make it all right, surely? If I take you to

dinner as a thank-you for making me the quilt, Dave couldn't complain at that, could he?'

If Dave were to understand what she was feeling just then, she thought bleakly, he'd certainly complain. But he didn't; and on Saturday Sean would be going.

'I suppose not.'

'Find a baby-sitter for Friday night, then. OK?'

On Thursday Emma called round at number nine to check the final measurements of the quilt border, only to find that Sean wasn't in. It annoyed her disproportionately, but on Friday she discovered why: he'd given himself a couple of days off after finishing the draft, and had spent part of that time buying more furniture for his house.

She had only been inside number nine once before, and then its spartan furnishings had left her unsurprised that Sean too seemed to prefer her house! But now the living-room boasted a leather chesterfield and two armchairs, as well as a growing library and a couple of Lillie's paintings on the walls, while upstairs Sean had a proper bed to sleep in.

It wasn't a brass bed, but the quilt looked very good set against the simple pine bedframe. However, the room was still far from over-furnished by Emma's standards.

'You could do with a proper wardrobe,' she remarked critically. 'And a bedside table, and a chair or two. Perhaps when this novel's accepted for publication. . .'

'Emma, love, it's not money that's the problem: it's just time and inclination. Even half a day buying furniture was more than enough for me. If you want me to get any more, you'll have to drag me to a shop and stand over me while I buy it.'

'I'll do that when you're back from London. Which reminds me, how long are you going to be gone?'

'I'm not sure.'

'You must have some idea.'

'Cool it, Em. Now I've got some phone calls to make. I'll come round at seven, OK?'

It wasn't OK: it annoyed her to be bustled out of the door by a short-tempered, oddly preoccupied Sean, when she'd been expecting to stay for a while and chat. It annoyed her, too, not to get a straight answer. Surely it didn't count as an invasion of privacy to want to know when he'd be coming back! What was more, it struck her, once she was back in her own living-room, that she had forgotten to ask him where they were going that evening.

With Dave she would have known what to expect, but with Sean she hadn't a clue. Nothing would have surprised her, from Tony's fast-food restaurant in the High Street to the fanciest French restaurant in Cowes. Thinking of that reminded her that Dave had phoned the evening before and suggested taking her to the latter that very night, and she had felt extremely awkward in putting him off.

She was starting to expect this ridiculous date to turn into a disaster, and it was in a foul mood that she hauled out her favourite peach jersey dress—after all, he hadn't so much as glanced at it when she had worn it to go out with Dave—and proceeded to bath and wash her hair. Chances were Sean would turn up in ancient denims and she'd feel ludicrously overdressed, she thought grouchily.

Duncan hovered around her while she was getting ready, grumbling that he didn't know what he'd do that weekend since Sean wouldn't be there to take him sailing, to play chess, or even to knock around a football, and she retorted with unusual venom that Sean wasn't his daddy, and he'd better not forget it.

Which brought Duncan to the edge of tears, and cost her a guilty half-hour in pacifying him. She was still finishing off her make-up when the doorbell announced, in quick succession, the arrivals of the baby-sitter and of Sean himself.

She left Duncan to let him in, and sat for a couple of minutes in her bedroom, hoping Dunc would come back up and tell her what he was wearing. She would have changed again, even now, rather than feel out of place all night. But Duncan's excited voice, wafting up the stairs, told her only that he still had far too much to tell Sean to bother with her. So she slid on her high heels and stumped downstairs—only to find Sean stretched out on the living-room floor, sorting out a tricky section of Duncan's Lego Technic model, and not only clad in his grey suit, but wearing a pair of newish, shiny, perfectly respectable black shoes.

'Good Lord!'

'What's up?' Sean murmured, not looking round. 'Won't be a minute, I'll just sort out these gears.'

'Your shoes.'

'Oh. Yes.' He did turn now, and gave her a devastating grin. 'You surely didn't imagine I'd take a lady out to dinner in my holey sneakers?'

'You went to Lillie's opening in them.'

'That was an artistic statement.'

'So what's this?'

'I'm not sure, quite.' He slotted a couple of pieces of Lego together, turned a tiny handle, remarked to Duncan, 'Should be plain sailing now,' then got to his feet.

'You should be grateful I'm not wearing my jeans,' Emma snapped, disconcerted.

'Now why would you do that? Anyway, you're not. You look lovely.'

'Thank you.' Dammit, she blushed. 'Where are we going?'

'I thought I'd make it a mystery tour.'

'Are you trying to make out you know the Island better than I do?'

'Only bits of it.'

He was right there, too. The main road from Newport to Shanklin was no novelty, nor was the turn-off to Ventnor, but when Sean started along the coast road from Ventnor to Shanklin and turned off that, she had to admit defeat. Until, belatedly, she recalled precisely when he had mentioned Shanklin to her, and realised that he was taking her to the Prince Regent. Which was a feat of deduction Silas South wouldn't have claimed much credit for, Sean pointed out, since they were by then almost within sight of the big country house hotel.

Of course Sean introduced her to Bob and Anna, his charming friends who ran the hotel, but he resisted the temptation to turn the evening into a propaganda exercise, and they sat down to eat without a single mention of quilting weekends.

It was a lovely meal. A melting fish mousse, served in a lobster sauce, was followed by truffled lamb with a purée of turnips and a fascinatingly varied salad. Agreeing that this wasn't the occasion to worry about her waistline, Emma allowed Anna to persuade her to a large piece of death-by-chocolate cake, which was even more luscious than it sounded, and by the time she and Sean were lingering over coffees and *petits-fours* she was feeling extremely pleased with the world.

'Not that I expected anything as grand as this,' she assured him, savouring a marzipan banana and glancing round the green and gold dining-room at the Prince Regent's undeniably affluent guests. 'I mean, with it being run by Bob and Anna, it's understandable you'd have chosen here, but. . .'

'You mean it wouldn't have done otherwise?' Sean sounded amused, but she sensed, too late, that she had been rather tactless and he wasn't far from being offended.

'Well. . . I mean. . .' she floundered. 'As a thank-you dinner. . .'

'Come on,' he said huskily. 'That was an excuse, and you know it.'

'Maybe, but you don't. . .You said. . .'

'Said what? That I'm not looking for heavy commitments? That doesn't stop me getting the best out of life, you know.'

'Of course not, but. . .'

'But what?' he persisted.

'But this *isn't* the best,' she said with sudden desperation. 'I mean, there must be someone—some special woman, somebody you want to. . .'

'No.' He reached out his hand, taking hers across the table, and fixing his sky-blue gaze on her. 'I wasn't seeing you as second best, Em. There's nobody I'd rather be with tonight.'

'Nor me. But——'

'Too many buts,' he brusquely interrupted, and Emma, meeting his eyes at last, realised that he had become just as tense as she, and was almost desperate to head off the conversation. 'Come on,' he went on, 'it's not yet dark outside. Let's walk down to the sea before we make our way back.'

She didn't argue. With half her mind she wanted to push him, but he clearly wasn't in the frame of mind to let himself be pushed. Anyway, what more could she have asked? Whatever her curiosity about his sex-life— or lack of one—he would undoubtedly have regarded that as none of her business. And he had made it clear enough that he didn't want to get involved in a physical relationship with her, so she wouldn't have dared press him in that direction, quite apart from the complication of Dave.

It still seemed to her, though, following a curtly abstracted Sean across the lawns of the Prince Regent, along the side of the tennis courts and down through trees to the head of the cliff, that their relationship wasn't *right*. There were men with whom she was capable of pursuing a relaxed platonic relationship, but Sean was emphatically not one of them. She couldn't help aching to be closer to him, and she was inclined to believe that he secretly felt the same way.

But how was she to make him admit that? She hadn't a clue. She reached for his hand as they stood gazing out to sea, but he let it slip out of her grasp—not rudely, but the message was clear enough. Anyway, what was the point? He was leaving again the next day.

Sean chatted with superficial ease on the drive back to Newport, and she roused herself to respond in the same vein, but he didn't touch her again before dropping her off outside number seven. Nor did he invite himself in, and after paying off the baby-sitter she went to bed feeling full, not only of rich food, but of a very uncomfortable kind of frustration.

CHAPTER SIX

'I MUST say,' Keith Frazer announced, storming into Emma's house at ten o'clock on Monday morning, 'I don't think it's on for you to send your friend round to us. If you're not happy with our agreement, you might have told us so yourself.'

'Sending my friend? I'm sorry, Mr Frazer, but I honestly don't know what you mean.'

'As if we're not used to the trade,' Mr Frazer hurtled on, without paying any attention to her remark. 'It's an insult, that's what it is. I'll tell you, my girl, Rose and I, we've been thirty years in the fancy-goods business— and there's not much you can teach us about it by now!'

'I'm sure there isn't,' Emma said hastily. With an effort she fought down her feelings of panic and dismay, and concentrated on soothing Mr Frazer down. Slowly she succeeded, until she had him seated in her living-room, his face fading from purple to its usual mottled red, and the kettle steaming its welcome.

Sean. She had guessed that even before Mr Frazer calmed down enough to explain; and his explanation, when it came, didn't surprise her that much. Except that she thought of Sean as an easygoing and even-tempered man, and he seemed to have come across very differently to the Frazers.

Was it really her laid-back friend who had 'marched' across to Seagulls and 'demanded' a written agreement on her behalf? Who had been 'aggressive' and 'rude' when the Frazers had indignantly refused to provide one? Who had even given them an ultimatum: no more quilts until an agreement was signed? She found it hard to believe, but Keith Frazer didn't mince his words, and his annoyance at Sean was certainly genuine.

As was Emma's, as the tale unfolded. How dared he? What was more, how dared he do it without consulting her, and without telling her afterwards? If she hadn't known he was in London she would have rushed next door and confronted him that instant.

But he *was* in London, and her first task had to be to mend relations with the Frazers, so she hurriedly reassured Mr Frazer that she was more than happy with his terms.

'I should think so too,' he belligerently agreed. 'Here's us doing you a favour, taking as much of your work as we can handle—and more!—and giving you the best terms we can afford. I can tell you, if we were the tight-fisted business people your "friend" seems to think we are, we wouldn't have taken ten of your quilts straight off, young lady!'

'I really didn't ask you to take more than you could cope with,' Emma nervously assured him. 'If you're short of storage space. . .if you'd like me to take some of them back, just until the shop's fully under way. . .'

'Oh no, I wasn't saying that. A deal's a deal, and we made one. *And* it doesn't need writing to make it binding.'

'Of course not.' Emma poured him coffee, and repeated her assurances again and again, until he finally admitted,

'That's a relief. We've enough troubles at the moment without you cutting up rough as well.'

'Troubles? What do you mean? The shop—it is going to open soon?'

'Not as soon as we'd hoped, but all's set now for the twenty-eighth of November.'

That was almost a month later than Emma had anticipated: bad news. But she couldn't do anything about it, and it wouldn't help to complain, so she expressed her relief that the date was now definite, and chatted politely as Mr Frazer downed his coffee.

Then she saw him out, and gave way to a scowl of annoyance. Curse Sean! All right, he wanted her to pursue his contacts, but that wasn't any excuse for messing up her existing arrangements.

She was still feeling miffed with him that evening, when Dave Madison called by to collect Ben who had been playing with Duncan after school—and mentioned that he had been hearing about Sean from the Morlands.

'I didn't realise he was that guy who'd been with you in the Wheatsheaf,' Dave grumbled.

'I did introduce you,' Emma pointed out.

'I know, but when you said about leaving Duncan with your neighbour, I thought you meant some old guy.'

'He's hardly that,' Emma conceded, 'but he gets on very well with Duncan.'

Dave assured her he didn't doubt that—but went on to point out that *he* got on well with Duncan too. And that it was understandable, surely, for a man in his position to feel a bit edgy when he heard that his girlfriend had been seen all around Newport—*and* at Carisbrooke, *and* on the road to Shanklin—with another man.

Yes, it was, Emma wearily agreed. She repeated that Sean was only a friend, but she had to agree that she had been seeing a great deal of him. And when Dave suggested that if she wanted to have a man around the house occasionally for Duncan's sake he'd be happy to oblige—bringing Ben as well, whenever he had charge of his son—she could only agree that that sounded like a good idea.

Dave took her at her word. He came to supper the following evening, then entertained Emma and Duncan to supper at his house on the Friday. On Saturday afternoon he and Ben, Emma and Duncan took the ferry to Portsmouth, and Dave and the boys went to see a football match while Emma shopped.

Dave and Ben were much in evidence on Sunday too, though that day went less smoothly, with Duncan and Ben squabbling over their morning football practice, and almost coming to blows over their Lego Technic in the afternoon.

It wasn't to be wondered at, Emma told herself. Given the exclusive attention of two adults Duncan thrived, but when he had to share them with Ben it was natural for a fair amount of rivalry to creep in. And although Dave did make great efforts with both boys his overbearing manner sometimes exasperated her, and she could understand why it didn't please Duncan much either.

'Mum,' Duncan said, when they were alone that evening—and finding it rather a relief—'when's Sean coming back?'

'I don't know, lovey.'

'I hope he'll be here next weekend.'

'Whether he is or not, we've agreed to go visiting with Dave and Ben on Sunday.'

'I'd rather have Sean here.'

'Well, he's not,' Emma said sourly.

In fact the longer Sean stayed away, the more exasperated with him she became. She suspected Duncan would be more enthusiastic about Dave if he weren't always comparing him—unfavourably—with Sean; and though she tried to resist the impulse she regularly found herself doing the same. When Dave shouted at the boys, or

annoyed them by trying to join in their game when he
wasn't needed, she would catch herself thinking that
Sean wouldn't do that.

Sean didn't bore her, and Dave did rather, now that
she saw so much of him. Nor did she really find Dave
sexually attractive, and while he was now pressing to add
a physical dimension to their relationship she was con-
sciously backpedalling in the opposite direction.

But what was the use of preferring Sean when he
wasn't around? She didn't have a choice to make between
him and Dave, because he had made it clear that he
didn't want to fill Dave's role in her life. He was the type
who would always be drifting on, always letting something or somebody else catch the bright gleam of his
interest, while Dave seemed seriously prepared to consider becoming a permanent fixture in her and Duncan's
life.

Wasn't that what she needed? All the stability a
Taurean asked for, she pointed out to Judy—and, when
Judy tartly responded that the complaints she had of
Dave all revealed his typically Arien nature, she tried to
laugh off the serious point she knew her friend was
making.

Dave spent another couple of evenings with her the
following week. She told him she would prefer to be
alone with Duncan on Saturday and catch up with her
chores, but on Sunday she kept to their plan to visit
some mutual friends who lived near Freshwater, in the
far west of the Island.

It was several months since Emma had seen Carole,
Michael and their children, and all of them thoroughly
enjoyed the day, sharing a huge lunch then enjoying the
glorious walk from Freshwater Bay up to the memorial
cross to the poet Tennyson on the downland beyond.

Emma and Carole had a chance to chat while the

children ran ahead, and Carole assured Emma that, although she was a little surprised, she was delighted to see her and Dave getting on so well.

Were they? If she was honest, Emma doubted whether she was fond enough of Dave to consider making their relationship permanent. She couldn't pretend to be passionately in love with him, and she guessed that he wasn't in love with her either.

But maybe it was asking for too much, to look for love in a second relationship? So many people seemed to settle for companionship, shared interests and shared responsibilities in bringing up their families: and Dave fitted that bill pretty well. He certainly seemed more suitable husband material than Neil had ever been, and had she really any right to expect more than that?

After all, nobody could have both security and wild excitement, she reminded herself, as she watched Duncan, Ben and Carole's son Tim chasing each other across the rough grass. With Duncan to consider as well as herself, surely her top priority had to be to establish a firm base to her life?

When Dave and Michael veered across to join her and Carole, she greeted Dave with a warmth that seemed to surprise him a little. But it pleased him too, as he made evident in giving her a quick hug and a snatched kiss, which the wind on the clifftop almost blew away from them.

The four of them were all contented, though windswept, as they made their way back to Newport. Emma had invited Dave and Ben for tea, and as soon as they reached number seven the boys rushed to Duncan's computer, while she and Dave retired to the kitchen to toast muffins and cut the cake she had made the day before.

'Expecting anyone?' Dave asked, when the harsh ring of the doorbell caught them by surprise.

'No.' But a jolt in the region of her heart said 'Sean'— and, of course, it was.

'You've been out for ages,' he announced, stepping inside without waiting for an invitation.

'Look who's talking! You've been gone over a fort-night!' she shot back, her voice given a sharp edge by the shock of seeing him. And shock it was, like plunging headfirst into cold water. Though they didn't touch, his impact was intensely physical, making her heart race and the blood surge through her body.

Before Sean could respond they were interrupted by Duncan, hurling himself along the hallway like a bullet.

'Sean, where've you been? You haven't been here for ages! Hey, we went to the football last week. We watched Portsmouth play Ipswich, and they won two-nil, and——'

'Dunc, that's great! Who scored the goals?'

His attention shifted to Duncan, sharp-edged as a searchlight beam, and for a moment Emma's frustration crested to such a peak that she was hard pressed to keep herself from physically intervening between the two of them. Ten seconds! Was that all he was allowing her?

It was ridiculous to be jealous of Dunc, she knew; but Sean *could* have told Duncan to run along, and concentrated on her. Then it struck her, in a sudden moment of ice-clear intuition, that he didn't dare. Their meeting had affected him in just the same way—and he was running away from his feelings, using Duncan as a soakaway for the emotion he didn't want to reveal to her.

'I've got a new computer game—come and see,' Duncan enthused, grabbing Sean's hand and hauling him off towards the living-room.

'Later, Dunc. I——' Emma began.

A touch on her arm made her jump, distracting her before she could put fully into effect her intention of holding Sean back. Dave. In the bare minute since Sean had arrived, she had completely forgotten he was there.

She spun round and glared at him; took in his frown, and realised belatedly that every one of her intense feelings must be clearly written on her face—and that Dave wouldn't take kindly to any of them.

If she couldn't completely hide her impatience to join Sean, at least politeness made her try to curb her annoyance with Dave. Which she did, though her efforts weren't helped by the sarcasm in Dave's voice as he remarked, 'I take it that's Davies?'

'Actually it's my friend Sean.'

'You didn't expect him?'

'Obviously not.' Whatever he'd seen and heard, he could hardly have failed to take in that much.

'I don't see why we should have him interrupting our tea-party. I'll tell him to push off.'

'You'll *what*?'

'Dammit, I'm not having him ruin our afternoon!'

Dave shoved past her, down the hallway and into the living-room. For an instant Emma froze; then she kicked her limbs into action, and hurried after him.

'Do you always burst into people's houses as if you own them?' Dave was demanding by the time she reached the doorway and paused, grabbing at the frame while she caught her breath.

Sean's eyes flicked from Dave to Emma, and held hers for a heart-stopping moment.

He couldn't hide his feelings then—they filled the space between them. Emma knew, with sudden joyous certainty, that he was in love with her.

And she was—— Good lord! How could it have happened? It was the last thing she had intended. But then, love never did depend upon intentions: it made its own rules. She could have spent a thousand years protesting that she hadn't meant to love Sean, that she couldn't handle him, that the sheer uncontrollability of her feelings terrified her, and it wouldn't have made a jot of difference. Without her even noticing, love had crept up on her, bound her fast and taken her prisoner.

'I can tell you it won't do,' Dave loudly persisted.

With an effort Sean tore his eyes from hers. He took a laboured breath, then regained his self-control, and said in a level—dangerously level—voice, 'Actually I don't make a habit of bursting into houses. I only do it where I know I'm welcome.'

'Well, you're not; not right now. Emma's busy.'

'Dave, please!'

'It's true, Emma. You invited us for tea, and I'm not having this character hijack it.'

'Dave!'

'Em, cool it,' Sean said quietly.

She didn't want to cool it! What she wanted was to get Dave out, immediately—ten minutes ago!—and be alone with Sean.

A vestige of sense told her, though, that force wasn't the way to achieve that. Dave might be arrogant, over-bearing and utterly wrong-headed in his possessiveness, but she couldn't actually frogmarch him to the front door, not when she *had* invited him to tea. However much she wanted him gone, he didn't deserve that.

The situation wasn't Dave's fault, even if he had made it worse by launching in with all guns firing for a contest that he was destined to lose. It was just bad luck on him, really, that he'd come up against a man who made him look small in every dimension. His attacking approach seemed like empty bluster, set against Sean's quiet control of the situation. His dark, dapper figure looked puny, contrasted to Sean's rangy power. Even his tweed jacket and trousers suffered in comparison with Sean's flamboyant outfit of checked jacket, fisherman's sweater and ancient denims.

It had to be love! Surely no woman with both feet firmly on the ground could have felt affection for Sean's red trainers, in which the hole had by now spread to crisis proportions.

Dave's only stroke of luck, really, was that Emma was too absorbed in Sean and her newly-discovered feelings to become as furious with him as she might otherwise have done. Sensing he'd lost out, he said sulkily, 'It's true. You did ask us, and you didn't ask him.'

'Talking of tea,' Sean said mildly, 'is that burning I smell?'

'Oh, gosh! The muffins!'

Emma dashed for the kitchen, which was rapidly filling with smoke, and hauled a tray full of cinders out from under the grill.

'Mum, what happened?'

'You can see what happened,' she muttered through clenched teeth. 'Go and play upstairs with Ben, love.'

'Has Sean got to go?'

'Yes. No. I don't know! Just clear off for a minute.'

'Aren't we going to have any muffins?'

'Doesn't look like it,' Sean's voice broke in. He reached a hand out over Emma's shoulder and gingerly picked up a burnt offering. 'In the bin, I think. And yes, I am going.'

'No, don't!'

'Be sensible, Em. We can't all sit round like a big happy family and munch these charred remnants. You sort things out with Dave, and I'll see you later.'

'I don't want you to go.'

'Nor do I, for what it matters. And I hope you tell

him to go take a running jump, but I don't see why that kid of his shouldn't have his tea first.'

'That's a point. You'll come round this evening?'

'After they've gone.' He touched her arm, glanced over his shoulder at where Dave was standing, glowering, in the doorway, then added, 'I'll let myself out.'

Which he did, leaving Emma to confront Dave.

'All right,' Dave said sullenly, 'I know that wasn't very tactful of me.'

Concern for Duncan and Ben made Emma swallow the vicious remarks that were shaping themselves on her tongue. 'Forget it,' she said brusquely, and busied herself cutting bread for toast to replace the wrecked muffins.

The four of them finished a subdued tea, then Dave and Ben left immediately afterwards. Dave didn't suggest seeing Emma again, and she guessed that he, too, knew that the incident had spelled out the end of their relationship.

When Dave had gone, Emma combed her hair, renewed her lipstick and waited for Sean. When he didn't come, she decided he was maybe having supper first. She played a desultory game of snap with a restless Duncan. Both of them kept glancing towards the front door, but the bell didn't ring.

Duncan suggested going next door for Sean. Emma told him not to. She guessed that Sean was waiting until Duncan was in bed. She shooed him into and out of the bath, overrode his protests that he wanted to wait up for Sean, and nagged him into bed.

Half an hour later he went to sleep. Sean still hadn't come. Emma made coffee, watched the television news, drifted restlessly from kitchen to living-room to hallway, decided Sean wasn't planning to come at all.

She phoned him.

Sean, sounding distant and offhand, said that a few work problems had come up and he'd see her soon.

'Tomorrow,' Emma said.

'Maybe,' he agreed.

Maybe? *Maybe*! She cursed his elusiveness to hell and back and went to bed, although it was long past midnight before she finally fell into a fitful sleep.

At eleven-thirty on a Monday morning when precious little work had been done, Emma gave up waiting and went round to number nine.

A tall, harassed-looking, unshaven figure opened the door to her.

'Oh. Hi,' Sean said vaguely.

'Well, thank you! You actually remember who I am!'

'There's no need to be like that, Em.'

'Yes, there is.' She stormed into his living-room and spun round to confront him. 'If I left it to you we'd carry on doing the lobster quadrille till our legs gave way!'

'The *what*?'

'You know the one. One step forward, two steps back.' Saying which, she took two very decisive steps forward, and wrapped her arms around him. 'Now don't run,' she said huskily.

'That'd be difficult, unless you had the three-legged race in mind.'

A splutter of giggles made her loosen her grip, though fortunately it didn't matter much, since by then he was holding her too. 'No, seriously,' she went on when she could trust her voice again. 'You accused me of being afraid, but I'm inclined to think you're worse than I am.'

'Am I running?' Sean asked in injured tones.

'Last night you did.'

He released her abruptly, and strode past her towards

the window. 'Em, be reasonable,' he said after a moment
of heavy silence. 'Neither of us really wants this.'

Her heart sank like a stone. His back was set to her in
a horribly unpromising way. But she fought back her
fear, and asked levelly, 'Wants what?'

He shrugged, his back still to her. 'An affair. A heavy
relationship. Commitment. Being trapped.'

'You think those are all the same?'

'Not always.'

'But for us? You and me?'

'Maybe.' He turned back to her, and held her eyes for
a moment, his look wide and blue and troubled. 'Em,'
he said awkwardly. 'You know how I feel.'

'No, I don't,' she said quietly. 'I don't understand
you—you're so different from me in some ways. I'm not
even sure what I want, let alone what you want. But
when you talk about being trapped. . . Sean, we still
barely know each other.'

'So you want to fall off a cliff. So you kid yourself that
we'll both decide to stop at the same place, and we'll be
able to stop. In mid-fall. I can tell you, it won't work
like that.'

'Couldn't it?'

He shook his head, and gave a wry smile. He paced
towards the chair furthest from where she was standing,
and threw himself into it, kicking out his long legs in
front of him.

'Em,' he repeated. 'All right, I want you. I want to
make love to you: I've wanted that ever since I met you.
But it's no good pretending that we could have a fun
affair and then go our separate ways with no hard
feelings. That's not how it is between us.'

'Then couldn't we have more?'

'There's a price to be paid for that, and I don't want
to pay it.'

'Being trapped,' she repeated, in a voice that tried to hide her hurt, as she claimed a chair herself.

'Yes,' he agreed. 'All right, that's maybe not what you intend, but that's what would happen.'

'No.'

'Yes,' he repeated, more vehemently. 'Look at it like this. There's a pattern by which you try—as everyone does—to run your life, and you try to cut and trim people to fit it. Like a quilt, in some ways. I could see you'd been doing it with that guy Dave. You must have known all along that he wasn't the right-sized stretch of cloth for the pattern you wanted, but you kept on trying to make the pieces fit on him. A bit of me wanted to shake you yesterday, to make you see he wouldn't do. But another bit of me thought, lord, if she sees that, she'll be trying her template out on me instead.'

'Couldn't you try *your* template out on me?' Emma asked unsteadily.

'I could; in a way I have been doing, but my pattern isn't the same as yours. Yours is that awful female pattern with a huge gap in the middle. Mine isn't like that. Mine's a Log Cabin sort of pattern, lots of little pieces intersecting.'

'How pretty,' she said with pained sarcasm.

'It suits me. OK, the pieces don't always fit together perfectly, but there aren't any gaping holes that I'm looking for someone to fill.'

'So what are you offering me? One tiny bit of your pattern?'

'Em, that's all I *have* to offer.'

'And you expect me to break with Dave, just so I can be a little oblong piece of your patchwork life?'

Sean slowly shook his head. 'I didn't say that, Em. I try not to expect anything of anyone, just as I don't like people expecting too much of me. You've a right to settle

for Dave if you think he fits well enough; I'm not asking
you to not do that for my sake. All I said was, it looks to
me as if he doesn't fit.'

'And nor do you,' she almost whispered.

'I guess that's true. I wish I did, but I don't.'

Silence. Outside the window, the gulls were wheeling
over the River Medina. An ice-cream sign outside the
Arts Centre clacked to and fro in the breeze. The sun
shone.

'I need a centre to my life, Sean,' Emma said painfully.
'I know what you're trying to say, but—you're wrong.
Life isn't exactly like a patchwork quilt. It needs more
than surface harmony, it needs depth. It needs a loving
relationship. You might call that awful, but most people
agree with me, men *and* women.'

'True. I'm the odd one out.'

'You wouldn't even try. . .?'

'Trying's not the point. You can't squeeze and stretch
people to be what they're not.'

'People change, though. People grow.'

'Em, don't. Please. You'll only hurt yourself. I'm just
not a marrying kind of man, and it's no good kidding
yourself that I am.'

'You've made that clear enough.' Her limbs felt stiff
with hurt as she got to her feet again. She knew what he
was saying, and she could see the sense of it, but. . .

But. He was right, there *was* a hole in her life, a huge,
gaping hole, and she did have a frightening hunger to
find somebody to fill it.

Not somebody. Sean.

Sean talked as if life was so controlled, as if people
chose their own pattern, but it seemed to her that life
wasn't like that at all. You didn't choose all the pieces of
your pattern. Your heritage, your temperament, the

people you loved, all came ready-shaped, and all you could do was to try and fit them in as best you could.

It seemed to her then that her life would be a wretchedly threadbare and shapeless affair if he wasn't there to give it meaning.

At that moment she hurt too much, though, to think of begging or pleading or pushing him. She sleepwalked towards the door, and her hand was on the handle before his voice held her back.

'Before you go, there's something else.'

'It'll have to wait,' she said tightly; then his door was open, and she was escaping into the coldness of the street.

CHAPTER SEVEN

RUN away Sean might, but next-door neighbours had their own spaces to fill in life's pattern; and Duncan, too, had his own ideas on where Sean belonged in his life. All Emma's insistence that he not knock on Sean's door fell on deaf ears. What was more, it opened to him when he went round after school that afternoon.

Emma stayed at home, working on a new quilt for an hour or so, then drifting downstairs to cook a beef casserole. It would feed three, if need be; if not, the remains could always go in the freezer.

Sean did follow Duncan in when he returned at six, but only to politely refuse her offer of supper. 'Although we do need to talk,' he added in a low voice, once Duncan had run off to wash his hands.

'What about?'

'The Frazers. Not in front of Duncan. Ring me when he's asleep tonight and I'll come round then.'

'If you're apologising for interfering, we'll take it as read.'

'Apologising!'

'Look, Sean——'

'Later,' Sean responded firmly.

By the time Duncan was fully asleep it was more than three hours later, and Emma's temper had risen considerably higher. Sean owed her an apology for rubbing the Frazers up the wrong way, and after that morning she felt entitled not merely to ask for, but to demand one. If he didn't want a place in her private life, then he had no right to interfere with her working life!

She stated all this very emphatically as soon as he returned, but it didn't have the effect she expected. It seemed Keith Frazer hadn't exaggerated: when Sean had fixed his mind on something he could indeed be forceful, aggressive and downright unswervable.

He pushed aside all Emma's claims that her main priority had to be to keep the Frazers sweet; on the contrary, he insisted, she needed to concentrate first of all on making sure she had a watertight deal with them. Trusting and hoping they'd play fair by her wasn't enough, when she was in a situation where a let-down could drag her under. She *needed* the security of a contract, and if the Frazers had been reasonable people they would have given her one—or rather given him one, when he'd asked.

He was briskly dismissive of Emma's suggestion that he had been rude and offensive to the Frazers. He knew how to negotiate a contract, he pointed out; he did it all the time for his literary clients.

'And don't tell me you know your customers better than I do,' he raged on, 'because it's not true, Em. I've had a dozen authors pull that line on me, and they've almost all been wrong. Not many people are hard-headed enough to negotiate properly when it's their own work at stake. Instead of treating it like a business deal, they trail around feeling *grateful*. Grateful! For being ripped off!'

'The Frazers haven't ripped me off!'

'No? You just wait!'

'Now look here,' Emma retorted, her temper fired now to boiling-point. 'It's all right your being so high and mighty about it, but don't you forget what a mess I was in before the Frazers came along. All right, I was grateful! But why shouldn't I have been? If *you'd* hawked your work all over the Island, and Southampton too, without stirring a flicker of interest, *you'd* have been grateful for their offer!'

'Not till they'd paid me I wouldn't have been.'

'They will!'

'Don't bank on it!'

'You—you cynic!' Emma screeched. Her resolution to keep a room's width between them forgotten, she hurled herself at Sean. Fingernails, fists, elbows, feet: she'd have used any weapon to hand, to punish him for what he was doing to her. She had started that day bright with optimism, and in a few fraught hours he had killed it all, attacking her on every front.

'Em!' Momentarily Sean flinched, then he moved on to the offensive. It was a moment's work to trap her hands in his. She twisted wildly, trying to get in a kick where it would hurt, but his strength was too much for her, and before she had managed to inflict more than a couple of bruises she found herself firmly pinned against the kitchen counter by the solid weight of his body.

'Em love,' Sean said tautly. 'Don't fight me. I'm on your side.'

'A funny way you have of showing it!'

'Give me a chance and I will.'

'You've had your chance, mate!'

With all the strength she had left she thrust herself forwards, launching into him; but he absorbed her effort easily, and it was she who fell back, shaken by the impact that the feel of his body, pressed hard against hers, had had on her.

Curse it. She wanted to be strong, wanted to do without him, but the sight, the feel, the smell of him were working a magic that neutralised all her strength. He seemed to feel it too, because even as her arms ceased to push against his restraining hands, his hold turned from a grip into an embrace.

She shuddered as his arms came round her, hating the intensity of the longing that would have caused her to forget her anger if only he'd make love to her. For a fraught moment he seemed to be as powerless against the urge as she was. His head bent down to hers, and she felt the warmth of his breath on her face. Her lips parted in anticipation of the kiss that he surely couldn't resist. . .

It didn't come. He released her abruptly, leaving her slumped against the counter. 'Now listen,' he said, his voice cold and harsh. 'I didn't mean to tell you all this— I thought it might panic you unnecessarily. But if you won't be sensible without knowing, then you'll have to know. I wouldn't accuse anyone without good reason, Em. I wish I hadn't cause to suspect the Frazers, but I have.'

She was beyond stopping him, beyond doing anything but listening silently as he rapped out the damning information that he had uncovered.

His suspicion, he explained, had been aroused when the Frazers had responded so aggressively to his perfectly reasonable request for a contract. Feeling sure they had something to hide, he had made it his job to learn more about them and their operation, making enquiries first on the Island, in the couple of days before he had left for London, and afterwards in the capital itself.

What he had learned in London had been enough to make him deeply worried. It seemed the Frazers hadn't simply retired from their gift-shop business in the Northeast, as they had implied to Emma: it had gone bankrupt. However, there had been worse to come.

That very day he had had a phone call from a potter acquaintance of Celia, the craft-shop owner who had bought Emma's quilts. As one of the Frazers' suppliers, she had suffered badly from the collapse of their business. But what had really upset her—and Sean, when he learned of it—was the way in which the collapse had been handled.

'When the receivers were called in,' Sean explained, 'Julie and the other craftspeople who'd supplied work were treated as unsecured creditors. Once other debts had been paid there wasn't any money to pay them for their work that had been sold, and some of them didn't even manage to reclaim work that hadn't been sold. They all lost out badly—but the Frazers didn't. They'd used all sorts of legal loopholes which meant that they emerged from the whole mess very comfortably off.'

'You mean they conned Julie?' Emma asked in an unsteady voice.

'Legally, no—but morally, I reckon that's a fair way of summing it up.'

'It won't happen again, though. Surely it won't.'

'Bankruptcy? Maybe not. But what you can't get around, love, is the fact that the Frazers are greedy and unscrupulous. They're only out for themselves: they have no principles, no sense of fair play. Anyone who supplies them needs to allow for that, otherwise they're likely to find themselves up the creek.'

Emma sighed. 'You're. . . I. . . Oh, damn it!'

'I know,' Sean agreed, more gently. 'I'm not expecting gratitude, Em: nobody likes being brought bad news. It's your lynchpin contract, and sure, you don't even want to think about it coming unstuck. But I couldn't leave you to carry on blind, knowing what it might mean in the long run.'

'So what do I do?'

'It's hard to say. Tread carefully.' He gave a tight grin. 'Watch your back. I'd say, go over to Seagulls and demand that contract, but frankly I don't rate your

chances of getting one where I failed, and it won't help
any if you make enemies of the Frazers. But don't rely
on them too heavily, love—and don't give them any
more quilts without a cast-iron agreement in writing.'

'How do I get that out of them?' she mused out loud.

'I'll do it. I'm thick-skinned.'

'Are you?'

'In my way.' He reached out and touched her cheek
with a long finger, brushing back a stray strand of hair
then lingering to caress the smooth skin that stretched
across her cheekbone. 'It's a downer, isn't it?' he said
gently.

She nodded. 'Just when I thought things were going
better. I was starting to hope everything was panning
out at last, my life was taking shape again, and. . .'

Her voice trailed away. Sean let the silence grow for a
while, then he said quietly, 'You're thinking about
Dave?'

'Dave!' She choked back a laugh. 'No,' she said
vehemently, 'I am *not* thinking about Dave.'

'But you feel the pattern's falling apart.'

'Yes and no. I haven't really fixed on a new pattern
for my life, and things with Dave never got to that stage
anyway. It's just that—there are good things in my life,
good friends, Duncan, work, but you're right, there are
some gaping holes too. They scare me, so I guess it's no
wonder they scare you as well.'

'Em, I. . .' He faltered, then took a deep breath and
began again. 'I'm not deserting you. You and Duncan
mean a lot to me. It's easy to say we're heading for
disaster and we'd do better to get out of each other's
lives, but I can't do it just like that. Even if I weren't
next door, I doubt if I could. I *want* to keep an eye on
you, and make sure you don't get out of your depth, and

see a bit of Duncan. But don't push me. Because when I feel I'm being pushed, I don't think; I back away fast.'

'So I've noticed.' She stood there for a moment, very conscious of his tall body a bare foot away from hers, and of the fingers that were now absently twisting strands of her hair.

He might be quicksilver in her hands, but there was a strength to him, she thought to herself. Elusive, yes, but he wasn't unreliable. And behind the scenes, unasked, sometimes unthanked, he'd relaid the foundations of her working life, planting healthy seeds and attacking the weeds that she had failed to see encroaching. It was a lot to be grateful for.

She shouldn't have risked it; she couldn't afford to lose it. But, standing here like this, the longing for all that he *wasn't* giving was stronger than she could bear.

Not to push, but just to move a step closer. . .

Her hand led the way, tracing a tentative path across his striped jumper, from his chest to his shoulder, where she let it rest more heavily, savouring the hidden strength underneath. Then her body followed, swaying forward so that her breasts just brushed against him.

He'd frozen, hand still tangled in her hair. Alarm bells were ringing in her head, but it wasn't calculation, it was sheer desire that moved her forward again—this time to stay.

Every nerve-ending was searingly alive. She was conscious of every point of contact between them: his shoulder muscles under her hands, the ache in her breasts, squashed against the hard wall of his chest, the strength of his thighs against hers.

'Em. . .'

'Just hold me. Please. Please, I won't ask for more. Just hold me for a minute.'

'Don't push me.'

'Just for a minute. Then you can go.'

She was holding her breath, tensed ready for him to push her away, but instead she felt him relax imperceptibly under her hands. Seizing the instant, she slipped her hands right round to his back, and brought her face up to his.

'This is crazy,' Sean whispered.

'It's what we need. Both of us.'

It was food to her hungry soul, the light prickle of his stripy jumper against her chin, the stubbly feel of his cheek brushing against her forehead, the warmth and faint spicy smell of him. No, it was champagne—on an empty stomach, going straight to her head, driving out the last doubts and inhibitions, leaving nothing but the urge to make him hers.

He didn't resist her as she pulled his head the last few centimetres down to hers. Her lips just touched his, thistledown-light. Then she felt the shift and stir of his muscles as he took control.

He'd relented this far, but his self-control was still intact, each movement judged. His lips barely settled on her skin before he moved on, touching her lips, the tip of her nose, teasing the tension out of her eyelids and jawbone. His tongue licked her lips apart, caressing the soft inner surface, sending pleasure flowering through her body. She responded with mindless, urgent delight, her hands roving across the expanse of his back, her breasts swelling tautly in response to the ache of contact. Then his mouth claimed hers fully.

It was a kiss not of reassurance, but of passion: a passion that she knew instinctively held them both, as she relaxed into the sweet flood of it. It contained no teasing, no fencing, no judgement: his lips didn't stray, his tongue didn't taunt. He met her desire head-on, his arms tightening around her.

One kiss, she had begged, but he barely paused to draw breath before kissing her again, and again, his masculinity as rawly unleashed now as it must have been in his confrontation with the Frazers. His hands caressed her in long strokes, moulding her body to his, as she moved in an increasingly purposeful rhythm against his swelling hardness.

'Em, what you do to me,' he murmured brokenly, his mouth searing a path from jawbone to neck, then searching out the pale smooth skin below the collar of the blouse he was fumbling to unbutton. He brushed aside the filmy cotton of her bra, and dropped hot kisses on the sensitive mound of her breast.

By the time his mouth found the hardened stem of her nipple she was dizzy with pleasure, her body arched back against the kitchen cupboards, her hands caressing the rough silk of his hair and the muscled firmness of his neck, shoulders and back. Her breath was coming in shallow gasps, her body raging for the fulfilment that it had been denied for so long.

The ringing in her ears seemed just another dimension of the torrent of feeling that was overwhelming her—until Sean raised his head and said, 'Do you want to answer it?'

'Answer. . .? Oh, gosh! The telephone!'

It was the last thing she wanted, but ingrained habit made her take a step forward, and Sean drew back as if he was expecting her to complete the movement.

So she did. It wasn't an urgent call, just one of her quilting class calling to tell her she couldn't make Thursday evening. Cursing her own conscience, Emma jotted down a note, thanked Amy, then rang off and turned to confront Sean.

He was standing in the doorway, still wearing the jacket he hadn't taken off since his arrival.

'Em, I'm going,' he said brusquely.

'Sean. . .'

'All right. No apologies, no post-mortems. And I'll come round tomorrow, I promise.'

Stay now! her heart screamed silently. But the moment had gone, and she knew he wouldn't be persuaded. She saw him to the door, then slumped down in her living-room and stared blankly at the window. How was she to survive this, and how would it end? She had no idea.

Sean was as good as his word. He *did* call round the following evening and stay for supper, although he made no mention of their lovemaking. Emma guessed he was regretting it. A part of her regretted it too, but another part defiantly refused to be sorry. It seemed the right, the only way for their relationship to develop, and she suspected that Sean knew that just as well as she did.

Still, she didn't dare to push him any harder, and over the next few days he always visited when Duncan too was around, effectively ensuring that she wouldn't have any opportunity to do so. She had to be content with enjoying his friendship; and although he didn't appear as frequently as he had done before his last departure he did spend several suppertimes with her and Duncan.

Things took another welcome small turn for the better a couple of days later, when Sean brought round a bottle of wine and the news that his friend Celia had sold both of Emma's quilts. 'I asked her if she'd pay up quickly,' he continued, 'and she promised to put the cheque in the post today. So the bank manager's not going to blacklist you this week—and you can see about sorting out another three quilts, please, Celia said.'

'Three?' Emma mused out loud. 'That'll leave me short, Sean, if the Frazers ask for any more.'

'I thought you'd given them ten?'

'True, and I'm inclined to think that will do them until February or March, but I did promise them up to forty a year. All right, I've taken in your warning but an agreement's an agreement. If I really insist, it's entirely possible that they'll sign my written terms, and then I'll have no excuse to break the agreement. And now we've fixed the quilting weekend I'd like to keep a couple of quilts to offer for sale there——'

'You've dozens upstairs.'

'It may seem so to you, but it's not that many. Take out the antique ones and my own competition winners, which I really don't want to lose, and there are only six or seven saleable quilts. Say, three in hand for the Frazers, two for the weekend, and that'll mean I can't send Celia more than two until I've made some more.'

'That's leaving you very dependent on the Frazers.'

'I know,' she replied tersely. 'It worries me too, but in the short term I've no option.'

Sean frowned, but he evidently saw the logic of her calculation, and he didn't push her to amend it. She handed over two quilts to him, with a promise of more as soon as she had them made, and he agreed to take them up to London when he next went there.

'Emma,' Judy said, on the phone a day or two later, 'we've made a snap decision to have a party for Guy Fawkes night this year. Have you made any plans? Can you and Dave come? And Duncan, of course.'

'Duncan and I can, but I'd rather not ask Dave,' Emma responded. She quickly filled Judy in on the teatime incident, explaining that she hadn't seen or heard from Dave since.

'I can't say I'm sorry,' was Judy's brisk rejoinder, and she calmly converted the invitation to, 'Bring Sean,' instead.

'I'm not sure he'll come, Judy,' Emma warned—adding that though Sean was very definitely around again it would be a mistake for Judy to see him as the substitute for Dave in her life. But she agreed to ask him, and in fact he proved enthusiastic, reminding her that he had been looking forward to meeting Judy.

Saturday morning brought a second, more panicky phone call from Judy. It was years since she and Tom had done a big bonfire, she moaned, and she'd forgotten how much work it was. Was there any chance of some help?

Duncan was at Sean's house, and Emma had been meaning to sort the fabrics for a Carolina Lily quilt, but she didn't like to leave her friend in the lurch, so she agreed to retrieve him and come to help for an hour or so.

'Don't be silly,' Sean said sharply, when she explained this to him a few minutes later. 'You told me you needed this as a working morning.'

'I know,' Emma retorted, 'but Judy needs help.'

'Is it for cooking?'

'I don't think so—just bonfire-building and getting the fireworks ready.'

'Then Dunc and I'll go over. Dunc, you know the way?'

'You don't *know* Judy and Tom.'

'I soon will,' Sean rejoined, grabbing jacket and scarf, and tossing Duncan his.

And that was certainly true. Judy rang again at lunchtime, complaining that if she'd known Sean was as nice as *that* she'd have made Emma introduce them weeks before, and warning Emma that she couldn't expect to see either him or Duncan before the evening. 'Sean and Tom have worked out a fantastic programme for the fireworks,' she explained, 'but it's going to take

them a while to get it ready. So I'll feed Sean and
Duncan lunch and supper, and you just bring yourself
over at seven. Right?'

'I haven't much choice, have I?' Emma commented.
She was smiling when she set the phone down, having
heard Sean's voice raised in good-natured argument in
the background, and so much laughter that she felt quite
lonely not to be part of all the fun. But the extra working
time was a godsend when she was so busy, and she made
the best of it, only stopping to change into warm clothes
at six-thirty, and to throw an extra sweater and scarf for
Duncan into her bag.

It wasn't a large party, just four families, but with an
average three children apiece that was enough to crowd
Judy's and Tom's back garden. Towards the foot of the
long narrow garden was a huge bonfire with a guy on
top—and leading from it, Emma noted with curiosity,
what looked like a clothes-line, the other end of which
was fixed high up an old chestnut tree about fifteen feet
away.

'Is that to stop the bonfire falling over?' she asked
Sean.

'No, that's for our grand opening.'

'What happens?'

'Wait and see,' he said, grinning.

Warmly dressed in thick denims and a blue donkey-
jacket, with his red scarf slung around his neck and his
trainers replaced by ancient wellingtons, he looked like
an eccentric farmer. A smear of mud branded his left
cheek, and underneath it was an angry scratch—sus-
tained, he explained, when he and Tom had been
hacking away at old brambles to clear a space around the
bonfire. But the prospect of the fireworks had put an
unholy gleam into his eyes, and, glancing around the
garden shed at the hastily carpentered frameworks of

sticks and old boards to which patterns of Catherine wheels and Roman candles had been fastened, Emma guessed Judy hadn't been exaggerating when she'd promised the programme would be fantastic.

Duncan came over to hold her hand for the start, as Tom and Sean shooed both adults and children to the top of the garden. Then, as Emma watched with fascination, Sean began to climb the chestnut tree.

'You see,' Duncan explained excitedly, 'he's going to light a rocket, and then it's going to go whoosh down the string, and right into the middle of the bonfire where Tom's put the paraffin, and then it's all going to burst into flames and set off that big rocket next to the guy.'

'That sounds absolutely——'

There was a fearsome screech and crash—the screech from the rocket, the crash from Sean, landing heavily as he jumped out of the tree. In a flare of light, the rocket screamed down the string, into the bonfire—and out the other side! It buried itself in a patch of nettles, and exploded in a chaos of sparks.

Emma's sentence was lost in a gale of laughter, from her, Judy, Sean and everyone else except for a harried-looking Tom, who was muttering something about 'bloody stupid bright ideas' as he cast around for a taper so that he could light the bonfire more conventionally. Sean, still unsteady with hilarity, found him one; the paraffin flared, the dry wood of the bonfire crackled into life; and behind the dark silhouette of the guy the second rocket took flight and soared high, high into the sky, overarching the scene with gold, blue and silver stars.

'All right,' Sean murmured. He'd joined the audience when she wasn't looking, and caught Emma from behind with two thickly clad arms. 'Not entirely what I planned, but still quite safe. And you wait: the rest will go perfectly.'

And it did. As soon as the guy had toppled and the
fire began to crumble into glowing embers, Judy brought
around trays of mulled wine and fruit juice. Then the
children drew pictures of light with their hand-held
sparklers, and then came the main firework display, a
dazzling triumph from the first set-piece, spinning
Catherine-wheels creating intersecting circles of fire, to
the grand finale of three double-decker rockets, chasing
each other into the sky.

While the garden was still warm from the fire they
remained outdoors, eating hot-dogs, hamburgers and
baked potatoes, drinking more wine, and chatting. Then
the younger children were carted off to bed, and the
adults and older children retreated into the house.

'I'd better take Duncan home,' Emma said—only to
have Sean firmly talk her down.

'Dunc's far from dropping,' he pointed out, 'and it's
Sunday tomorrow. A single late night won't hurt him.
Relax; wait till he asks to go home, and enjoy yourself.'

Actually she herself was probably more tired than
Duncan was, Emma thought ruefully. Being weary,
though, made it even easier to give in to Sean's persuading and sit next to him on Judy's big squashy sofa,
sleepily half listening to him arguing politics with Tom
and his friend Jeff.

Eventually she fell into a doze, and the next thing she
was conscious of was Sean gently shaking her awake,
telling her that it was past eleven. He'd already settled
Duncan in his car, and was firmly dismissive of Emma's
suggestions that she take her own car home. She was far
too tired to drive, he insisted, and would do much better
to let him return her to collect it in the morning.

And he did just that, dropping her once more at Judy's
house twelve hours later.

'Where's Duncan?' Judy's sons Pete and Eric chorused.

'He's driven off with Sean; they're going to Cowes, to do some work on his boat.'

'We thought he'd help clear up the garden.'

'Oh—I should have thought of that. I'm here, though—I can help you do it.'

'No, you'll help me in the kitchen,' Judy insisted.

There was plenty of clearing-up after the party to be done in the kitchen, but Judy's main motive was to talk, as Emma had no difficulty in guessing. Nor was she surprised when Judy launched in on the subject of Sean as soon as they were alone.

'Not a substitute for Dave, indeed!' she said indignantly. 'You can't expect me to believe that, Em!'

'Jude, I wish he were—but he's not interested in that kind of relationship.'

'Oh, no? He talks about you all day, he hardly takes his eyes off you all evening, the two of you cuddle up on the sofa like an old married couple, this morning he takes Duncan——'

'Hold on! All right,' Emma continued, more lamely, 'that's true as far as it goes—but it doesn't go any further, Jude.'

'Any further! Em, how long have you known him?'

'Six, seven weeks.'

'So what do you expect? A proposal of marriage? Give the man time!'

'It's not a question of time.'

'Of course it is. Em, I know you're impatient; I know you don't like uncertainty and insecurity. You typical Taurean, you'd like to have all the changes in your life out of the way, so you can settle down into a nice comfortable new rut. But when you're dealing with an

Aquarian like Sean you have to let him take his own sweet time.'

'Oh, he does!' Emma agreed. 'But Jude, he's simply not heading in that direction. His path doesn't lead to a rut. He's hung up on freedom: no ties, no responsibilities.'

'Is he?'

'Don't sound so sceptical—you told me that! Earth people like me go for security, air people like Sean thrive on insecurity.'

'We-ell,' Judy said consideringly, 'there's something in that. But you don't have to take it as a fixed rule, Em. You may be a Taurean, but you've lived through plenty of upheaval, and emerged from it stronger. Similarly, Aquarians might like freedom, but that doesn't mean they always run away from loving relationships. In the end most of them let themselves be pinned down. They don't like to feel trapped, but they'll often settle for a cage with an open door.'

'Sort of—feeling free, rather than being free?'

'Sort of. Aquarians fall in love, just like everyone else, and when they do they feel the urge to share their lives. What they don't like, though, is to feel that their life has been taken over by someone. If you can persuade Sean that commitment to you won't stop him living life on a broad canvas, then I think you'll find him willing to make that commitment in the end.'

'I hope you're right,' Emma said fervently.

'So do I,' Judy agreed. 'I like him so much, Em. He's just the kind of warm, friendly, lively man that you and Duncan need. And disgracefully good-looking, too!'

'Maybe too good-looking,' Emma ruefully pointed out. 'It's all very well your sounding so certain, but he's been a bachelor for thirty-four years, Jude, and I can't be the first woman who's thought of trying to change that.'

'No, but you might be the first he's really fallen in love with. You may say he's being evasive, Em, but it looks to me as if he's making a lousy job of running away from you. Just be patient. Don't grab, play him like a fish—an old and wily pike.'

'I'm no good at that kind of game.'

'Then learn,' Judy said tartly. 'It'll be worth it.'

CHAPTER EIGHT

SEAN stayed in Newport for another fortnight. He was working on the revision of his novel, a job that he took far less frantically than the first draft, allowing himself a generous amount of free time.

Although he'd now acquired a wide circle of friends in Newport, he didn't hide the fact that he preferred to spend that time with Emma and Duncan. His 'every other day' caution had been thrown aside, and as often as not he'd come over to number seven as soon as Duncan was out of school, keeping an eye on him while Emma worked, then staying till after supper or even later.

Judy, Tom and their other friends took it for granted that he and Emma were a couple, and as far as Emma could see Sean wasn't making any effort to correct that impression. He went with her to dinner with Marie and Ted; he drove her and Duncan over to Freshwater to visit Carole and Michael. The three of them ate out at a pizza restaurant, went for a long walk on a fine Sunday afternoon, and had a hilarious five-hour game of Monopoly on a wet one.

Lillie came down for a couple of days to collect the unsold pictures from her exhibition—which had done better than she'd originally feared, with more than half her work selling—and she and Emma cemented their friendship. Emma bit back her jealousy and said nothing when Sean and Lillie went out to dinner together, only to have Lillie complain afterwards that it might have been better if she *had* been there, since Sean had talked about her all evening!

He *was* in love with her. She didn't need Judy or Lillie to tell her that—although they both did—since she could read it for herself in his look, his smile, his occasional touch. But still he was holding back.

They weren't lovers. He didn't even kiss her again, and that didn't surprise her, since she knew that even Sean couldn't kid himself any more that a kiss would be 'just' a kiss. There were times when she felt she'd go crazy with frustration, and she guessed he felt the same. But she would have hesitated to take the initiative in lovemaking again, and in any case he was careful to avoid giving her opportunities to try.

Maybe it was true, as Judy suggested, that sex was her strongest weapon in the silent battle to tie him down. But it was also the weapon he was alert to, and that held her back from using it.

Anyway, it wasn't her only weapon. Every minute and hour he spent with her and Duncan, every mutual friend they made, every thought they shared, served to thicken the thread that linked his life and hers. Already she saw more of him, and shared more with him, than she had done with Neil at any time during their marriage. She warmed herself on that thought, and held her other weapon waiting in readiness, until the pike rose closer to the surface and she had her chance to hook him.

The fortnight came to an end, though, with nothing changed. It didn't surprise her when Sean announced on a Monday evening over a game of Scrabble that he was going back to London the following day; really the surprise was that he had stayed in Newport so long. She knew now that he had never intended to move permanently to the Island, having bought number nine as a second home, a quiet retreat to use when he was hard at work on his books. He was spending far more time there than he had originally intended, though this was something he hadn't confessed directly to her: she'd learned it through Marie and Ted.

'Do you *have* to go?' Duncan grumbled.

'Yes, I do, lad. I can't do all my work from Newport. I need to see my editor, and to chase up a couple of contracts for the clients I have as a literary agent, and to talk to a man from the BBC, and——'

'But you'll be back soon?'

'As soon as I can.'

'Will you miss us?'

Emma blanched. Only nine-year-olds could get away with that sort of question! But Sean took it in his stride, smiling and saying wryly, 'Of course I will.'

'Why don't you phone us when you're in London?'

Sean didn't glance at Emma, but his voice was still reasonably level as he agreed, 'OK. This time I will.'

He left Emma a note of *his* phone number too, although she wouldn't have used it except in an emergency. And he did phone several times in the fortnight he was away, but she felt awkward about asking him what he was doing in London, and who he was doing it with, for fear her jealousy of this other life of his, the one she was excluded from, would come across too clearly.

Instead they talked mainly about friends and goings-on in Newport and elsewhere on the Island. The opening of the Frazers' shop was looming, and rather to Emma's surprise they were planning a formal launch party, to which she had received an invitation.

'If you'd like me to, I'll come back for it,' Sean offered, 'but I'm not sure it would be wise. I'd rather play your heavy man when you need one than pretend to be nice to the Frazers, and the party doesn't fit in easily with my work commitments. If I stay in London till the Friday of your weekend at the Prince Regent, I'll not only be down on the Island for that, but I'll be able to stay till almost Christmas.'

Then he'd leave for Christmas, Emma assumed. To go where? To London? To his family? She hadn't any particular plans for Christmas herself, and she had been hoping he'd be around over the holiday season. But she knew she shouldn't have expected that; and if he wasn't going to be in Newport she couldn't bring herself to ask where he was going to be.

'That sounds sensible,' she agreed, in the brightest voice she could manage. 'I'd have liked you to be at the Frazers' opening, but I can see the drawbacks. And Judy said she'd come with me, so I won't be thrown to the wolves! The important thing is for you to come down to the Prince Regent with me.'

'Of course; I know you need me to keep an eye on Duncan. That's firmly booked in my diary.'

Actually she had changed her plans about the weekend, and she didn't need him for that reason. But it would be better tactics, she decided, not to admit that quite yet.

The moon was in Taurus on Monday, November the twenty-eighth, a good omen for Emma, as Judy told her while they were driving the ten miles or so that separated Ryde and Newport. The 'challenging aspects' of a month or two earlier—Judy's professional term, for which Emma ribbed her shamefully—had given way to a calmer chart, and it looked as if her life really was settling into a new channel at last.

Typically, Judy had wormed a precise date and time of birth out of Sean, and she had prepared a full astrological chart for him and compared it to Emma's.

'You're a good fit,' she assured Emma. 'Though it hardly needs an astrologer to see that! Anyone with common sense would agree that he's good for you, and you for him too, but it's all there in your charts as well. Your sun signs don't make for the easiest of combinations, but the planetary positions in your two charts more than make up for that.'

'Give me some advice?' Emma asked. She outlined her plan for the quilting weekend, and Judy laughingly agreed that her psychology and her timing both looked to be dead on target.

'Thanks,' Emma said. 'Confidence makes a big difference, you know! I'm beginning to see now why you generally opt for optimistic forecasts. Tell somebody things are liable to go wrong, and it can turn into a self-fulfilling prophecy. While tell them the omens are good, and——'

'And they're halfway to getting what they want,' Judy agreed.

'You've been such a help to me, Judy. I think without your putting me right, I might have gone on for much longer thinking that Sean was just another Neil. On the surface they are alike in some ways—they both have a kind of easy friendliness that attracts me—but underneath they could hardly be more different. Neil was well-intentioned, but weak and selfish, while Sean's a sharing person. And surprisingly strong, when you get to know him.'

'I'm sure he is,' Judy agreed.

'Unlike the Frazers. Any advice there?'

'Not really. I thought you and Sean had that situation pretty well under control?'

'I'm on my guard now, and that has to be a good thing,' Emma confirmed.

By this time they were coming into Ryde, and it didn't

take her long to track down a parking place on the Esplanade and walk with Judy the couple of blocks to the gift shop, where the launch party was just getting under way.

The Frazers had called their shop 'Favourite Things'. It was well placed on the edge of Ryde's main shopping centre, and had an impressive double front. It was spacious inside too, and high-ceilinged, so that Emma's quilts were displayed on a clear expanse of wall above shelves full of smaller merchandise.

All this was a welcome discovery, and the launch party itself seemed to be a great success: the brightly lit shop was crammed with people. But when Emma took a closer look at the merchandise her heart began to sink.

It shouldn't have been a surprise to her that the Frazers' taste didn't match her own: her return visit to Seagulls had told her that. It hadn't occurred to her before, though, that their shop might be jam-packed with the kind of tasteless tat she had so disliked in their home.

A few of the craft objects were excellent, but when Judy whispered that she thought most of the stuff was a load of rubbish Emma could only agree.

'Still,' Judy hissed, 'it makes your quilts look fantastic by comparison. They've hung them well, too.'

Yes, they had. With the quilts set high on the walls it wasn't easy for potential purchasers to take a close look at her workmanship, but the designs came across beautifully.

In spite of Judy's reassurance, though, Emma couldn't help worrying about the general style of the shop. Really it seemed to be setting out to attract passing trade: tourists with a couple of pounds to spend on a souvenir of Ryde. Her quilts simply weren't that kind of impulse buy. They demanded an entirely different clientele, a shop with a different reputation. Selling forty a year? She'd be lucky if the Frazers sold one, she thought pessimistically.

Oh, well. She'd have to let the situation ride for a while, and then if they hadn't sold anything by Christmas that would give her an excuse to retrieve her work and offer it to Celia instead.

And, looking on the bright side, the opening itself was providing an opportunity for a roomful of people, several of them rich and influential, to admire her work. Judy also tracked down the reporter from the *Newport Herald*, whom she knew from her own work with the paper, and ensured that he interviewed Emma at length. So it wasn't a wasted afternoon, and after enjoying the canapés and drinks that the Frazers had laid on both Emma and Judy were reasonably cheerful by the time they extricated themselves and hurried back to collect their children from school.

It was a surprise—a big surprise—when Rose Frazer rang Emma on the following Friday, the eve of her quilting weekend, to announce that three of the quilts had been sold.

'Three of them!' Emma was speechless. All right, it was close to Christmas, the perfect time for buying presents, but still she hadn't expected that kind of success.

'Isn't it good?' Mrs Frazer said enthusiastically. 'I told you we'd shift them with no trouble.'

'It's—it's marvellous.'

'You'll know what I'm going to ask now.'

'How many more you can take?' Emma calculated rapidly. She had rather come to assume that the Frazers' shop was a write-off, and when she had last spoken to Sean on the phone she had half promised all her spare quilts to Celia, who was also making an excellent job of selling them. But her commitment to the Frazers had to come first, so she swallowed her reservations and assured Rose Frazer that she could collect the remaining quilts as soon as she could arrange to do so.

'Not this weekend,' she added, 'since I'll be away.' They fixed on Tuesday, and Emma rang off feeling dazed but delighted with the change in her fortunes.

'Missed you,' Sean announced, breezing into Emma's house that afternoon, and catching her up, to her surprise, in a warm bear-hug.

'Missed you too.'

'Did you?' His blue eyes held hers as he released her, narrowed in a sharp assessing way. 'I thought for a moment you'd found someone else.'

Someone else? Was he *jealous*?

If he was, she didn't dare to rub it in too hard. Lightly, she responded, 'I thought the idea was for us both to have lots of someone elses. A patchwork of friends, wasn't that your phrase?'

'Well. . .yes, but I do like to keep my place in the pattern.'

'You will,' Emma assured him. 'Anyway, what made you think that?'

'The car in your garage. It's hard to imagine you'd swap your old estate for a year-old BMW. And if I were the suspicious type,' he continued, eyes scanning her kitchen in a manner that rather implied he was, 'I'd be wondering about the bottle of champagne over there as well.'

'Would you, now? If you did just happen to be that suspicious type?'

'Must be Silas South coming out in me.'

She shook her head. 'Too obvious. Too blatant.

Champagne hidden in the larder, maybe, but champagne on the counter. . .'

'Em, be reasonable. I know there's a message in it, but I'm not *that* psychic.'

'It's really got you ratted, hasn't it?' She eyed him with growing amusement.

'So take pity on me, damn you!'

'Give me a kiss and I will.'

'That's extortion.'

'So it is,' she agreed.

'All right, then.' He slid his arms round her and dropped the quickest of kisses on her mouth.

But when he tried to pull away again she was ready for him, her hands on his jacket sleeves holding him back.

'Come on, Sean. A proper kiss.'

'You drive a hard bargain,' he groaned.

'Sure do.' She watched him from under her lashes, running her tongue across her suddenly dry lips. It was time to reel in her line. And the pike was hooked, but not landed yet—a thought that made her feel nervous but exhilarated.

Sean's sharp blue gaze was wary, but steady, as she opened her eyes a little wider, sought it out, and held it.

Her hands crept up his arms, as she narrowed the gap between them. She was stretched up on tiptoe, her body tense with the effort of keeping her movements light and confident.

Latent energy filled the pause. Then he snapped the elastic, pulling her tightly to him as his mouth hammered down on hers.

Oh, yes. Oh, yes, the wanting was there, she realised, fiercely exultant as he crushed her to him. Hers wasn't the only body that was throbbing with hunger, hers weren't the only urges that were aching to be given fulfilment. This bruising kiss was in itself a fulfilment, even if it awoke deeper and stronger desires within her.

But this wasn't the moment to relieve them, and she didn't protest when a moment later he released her. They stood there for a moment, recovering their equilibrium, then Sean said in a low voice, 'So now you owe me an explanation.'

'So I do. Actually it's all very simple. The car belongs to my parents: they've come to stay for a few days. And the champagne is a little treat for us all, because the Frazers have sold three of my quilts.'

'Three quilts! Good lord!'

'Isn't that good?'

Sean hesitated fractionally, then relaxed into a smile. 'I was going to say, "When they pay you it will be", but that'd be mean of me, wouldn't it. It's marvellous, Em.'

'It is. Such a relief.'

'What's this about your parents, though? You surely haven't forgotten about the Prince Regent?'

'Of course not; I'm all packed ready to go after tea. They'll be staying here without me, looking after Duncan.'

'But I——'

'I know you were,' she interrupted, 'but I thought better of that plan. Face it, Duncan really wouldn't enjoy a weekend in a luxury hotel, and when Mum and Dad suggested coming down for a pre-Christmas visit I thought this would solve all our problems. They're staying till next Wednesday, so they'll see plenty of me as well before they go.'

'A pre-Christmas visit? What's the point of that? You'll be seeing them at Christmas anyway, won't you?'

'Not this year.' Briefly, Emma explained that her parents planned to spend Christmas in Spain, so that this trip was meant as an opportunity to swap news and presents beforehand.

'Don't you mind not spending Christmas with them?' Sean queried.

'We spent last Christmas with them.'

'Maybe, but what will you do this year? You haven't any other close relatives, have you?'

'We'll stay here. I expect we'll have a good time.'

From Sean's frown, it was apparent that he didn't think much of this arrangement—and, to be honest, Emma wasn't enthralled by it either. She would have preferred her parents to play a larger role in her and Duncan's life than they did, but they had their own busy lives to lead, and had never shown themselves willing to up their level of visits from the two a year they'd set when Neil was alive. She suspected it hadn't occurred to them that she and Duncan might rely on their company over the Christmas holiday—and they would probably have been astonished and resentful if it *had* been suggested to them. Most likely, objecting to their plans wouldn't have resulted in their revising them, only in an awkward scene, so she'd resolved to accept them with a good grace.

Sean's opinion didn't make that any easier to do. But already he'd moved on, focusing instead on the question of Duncan, and the change in her weekend plans.

'Em, you might have told me you wouldn't need me this weekend.'

'But I do need you. Duncan doesn't, admittedly; but I do.'

She held her breath. And Sean made her wait—punishing her, she thought ruefully—until finally he muttered, 'Well, I'm still coming.' Then added, 'I'd better push off now, though, if you're expecting your parents back for tea.'

'Why, do you mind meeting them?'

'I hadn't expected it.'

'That's obvious. You've got to change before we set off, though, so why don't you do that now, then come back round for tea?'

'Change? Why?'

'That jacket's why.' She took in his almost comical expression, and went on, 'Yes, honestly. It won't do for the Prince Regent, and it's not designed to impress my mum and dad either. Really, love. Bohemian's fine, but dirty isn't. I mean, those checks might come up white if you had it cleaned!'

'I thought they were,' Sean said in injured tones. 'So what do you suggest? A suit?'

'*A* suit? You mean you've more than one?'

'Half a dozen, though they're not all down here with me. I could manage the grey one you've seen before, though; or just a jacket and trousers.'

'And tie? No—no tie, you'd feel uncomfortable. That shirt would do, with a different jacket and trousers. And hey, I like the trainers.'

'Real cool, huh?' He flexed one foot, respectably clad in holeless navy blue trainers. 'My editor dragged me out to buy them.'

And you let her? Emma marvelled.

Yes—yes, he would have let her, she suddenly realised; just as he'd let Lillie stand over him while he bought furniture for his house. Far from being offended, or even feeling trapped, he'd genuinely been pleased by their interest—and their willingness to help with a chore he hated!

Maybe she herself had been a little too unassertive up till now, putting up with his beyond-the-pale outfits when some tactful urging would have got him into something much more appealing.

'Tell you what,' she said slowly, 'I could come over to your house and help you choose what to wear. There's time: Mum and Dad and Duncan went for a walk by the river, and they won't be back for ages yet.'

He let her, too. Five more minutes found her sprawling across the Next-door Neighbour quilt on his bed, watching a jacketless Sean unzip his denims and step out of them. And watching was the word! She didn't even try to hide her interest, as he realised when he turned to glance at her.

'Which pair? The grey ones?'

'Mmm. Change your shirt too.'

'I thought you liked my shirt,' he jokingly protested, glancing down at the inoffensive expanse of cream brushed cotton.

'I'd like you more without it.'

'What is this? A fashion show, or. . .?' His voice trailed away, as Emma uncurled herself from the bed and stalked across the bedroom floor towards him.

'Let's do this properly,' she said seductively, reaching out for his wrist and proceeding to unbutton his shirt cuff. 'If you take it off, then I can decide whether you're better off wearing that one, or. . .'

'Sue didn't do this when we picked out my new trainers.'

'I should hope not.' She dealt with his other cuff, then turned her attention to the buttons down the front of his shirt. Mmm. Muscular shoulders that looked as good as they felt. A surprisingly thick mat of light brown hair on his chest, thinning out as she got down to a hard, flat stomach, and narrow hips part hidden by his red boxer shorts. She pushed his shirt back off his shoulders, and took advantage of the moment when his arms were trapped to move closer, pressing herself against the firm warm expanse of his body.

She dropped a kiss on his collarbone, then licked, experimentally, savouring the clean, slightly salty taste of him. Then gasped as he shook his hands free and caught hold of her around the waist.

'How long did you say we'd got?' he asked in a low, amused voice.

'Maybe half an hour.'

'Not long enough.'

'Not long enough for what?'

'What you and I have in mind.'

'Now what tells you what I——?'

'Detective work.'

His hands raked down her back, drawing her tightly to him, and his mouth firmly shut off any further discussion. Not that she could have pretended she didn't know what he meant, when both their bodies were responding to the intimate contact by overheating in all the predictable places.

Sean let the temperature rise a few degrees higher, his tongue, his hands, his jutting hips all reinforcing the message; then he put her away from him, and bestowed on her a slightly breathless smile.

'We could be late. . .' Emma murmured.

'Nope. Tonight, when there's no deadline. Now concentrate, woman. Which shirt with the grey trousers?'

Tonight? Tonight! So much for her elaborate plans to catch him—he wasn't even running away!

All the same it was an effort to give in to his injunction, and to keep her voice and manner casual as she helped him sort out a grey shirt and navy pullover to go with his grey trousers. She nodded approval of his navy blue jacket, then protested bitterly, and entirely without success, when he topped the ensemble with his favourite red knitted scarf.

'Be reasonable,' he insisted. 'I'm not an accountant!'

'Nobody would take you for one, I promise!' Although that would have been true even without the scarf, she thought privately. His unruly hair, the manic gleam in his eyes, the tigerish strength that characterised his loping walk, all proclaimed a man who didn't care to blend with the crowd.

Still, she did like to see him looking smart, and it pleased her even more when her parents were clearly taken with his appearance and his friendly manner. They enjoyed a very cheerful tea-party, only marred slightly when Duncan took a big gulp of Emma's champagne and was seized with an attack of hiccups, then Sean waited while Emma ran through her last-minute instructions for her parents. It was barely dusk when they set out—in Emma's estate car, loaded with quilts and quilting materials—across the Island to the Prince Regent.

The hotel was crowded with people taking a break from the rigours of Christmas shopping, but Anna had found Emma and Sean two lovely rooms next to each other, overlooking the sea.

Each touch, each look now seemed to be a confirmation that Sean had meant what he said earlier. He might still be harbouring some inward doubts, but Emma knew instinctively that he'd no more be able to sleep apart from her that night than she would be able to endure it if he did.

First there was work to be done, though. Sean helped her prepare the room that Anna and Bob had reserved for her course, setting out a display of quilts and smaller patchwork items, another of books and templates for sale, arranging bales of fabric and wadding, and assembling the big wooden quilting frame that usually half filled her workroom. Then Bob carried him off for a game of squash on one of the hotel courts, while Emma stayed to welcome the members of the course.

Though it had been arranged at fairly short notice the course had almost sold out, proving, to Emma's delight, to be one of the most popular that the hotel had run. Eleven women were gathered for the introductory session before supper. Some were beginners, but one or two were experienced quilters, and Emma had a busy hour and a half discussing the kind of work they hoped to do over the weekend.

Anna had assured her that she wasn't expected to spend every mealtime with her course members, but she guessed she'd have little option but to do so, to judge by their friendliness and their endless stream of questions. A couple of women were still waiting to talk to her when the group reached the dining-room, and though she saw Sean sitting across the room she couldn't do much more than gesture her apologies to him.

He'd expected to have Duncan's company, and for a moment she guiltily wondered if her careful plan was about to backfire, leaving him thoroughly fed up with a weekend when she was monopolised by quilters, and unable to spare him more than the odd minute. But when another man joined him at his corner table she realised she'd once again underestimated his capacity to make friends instantly, anywhere. In fact it was she who kept jealously glancing across to where Sean and his companion seemed to be having a whale of a time, chatting and laughing over the superb meal.

For a moment she resented having to return to the conference-room for another hour-long session with her class after supper. But really it was a pleasure to have the enthusiastic attention of women who shared her passion for quilting, and the demands of planning a weekend project for each woman successfully kept her mind from straying too often to Sean, and what might happen afterwards.

Ten o'clock approached, the end of the session, and the room was still humming with activity. Usually Emma had no trouble winding down her classes on time, but then her usual students didn't plan to complete major projects over a single weekend. She glanced surreptitiously at her watch, knowing that whatever her impatience it wouldn't do to offend her students by seeming over-eager to escape.

Her dilemma was solved when a knock at the door brought Sean himself into the room. 'Just thought I'd see how you were getting on, darling,' he explained, leaning over Emma's shoulder, and sharing with her a private glance which she hoped the other women present didn't read *quite* as accurately as she did.

'Oh!' one of the women expressed the thoughts of the others. 'We didn't realise your husband was——'

'It's all right,' Sean said with a smile. 'I'm not in that much of a rush to drag her away.'

For a while he circulated, chatting up a couple of the older ladies with his usual charm, and impressing them with his now considerable knowlege of quilting. But his interruption had had its intended effect on their social consciences, and in less than a quarter of an hour he and Emma were left alone in a room strewn with open pattern books, sketches on paper, and a profusion of bright fabrics.

'Looks fun,' Sean said thoughtfully. 'Perhaps I should have enrolled on your course myself.'

'There's room for one more.'

'Too late. I've fixed up another squash game, I want to try out the pool, and I've an article to draft over the weekend.'

'Sounds as if you'll have no time left for me.'

'There's now.'

'I thought you were going to bed now.'

'So,' he said dangerously, catching her to him, 'are you.'

'Sean, are you sure? I don't want you to feel I——'

'Em, did anyone tell you you're the most lousy seductress?'

She froze in his arms.

'Hey.' His hand caressed the back of her head. 'You ought to know that's not a rejection. But honestly! Three months to get into bed a man who's been crazy about you since the minute he first saw you!'

'It's not for lack of wanting to,' she whispered.

'I know. You're just a hopeless saleswoman, with the most marvellous goods on offer, and too shy to push them properly. Didn't anyone warn you never, ever to offer the customer a let-out at the last moment?'

'I didn't see it like that. Really, I wasn't——'

'Not plotting? Not planning? Come *on*. Who got Duncan out of the way and didn't tell me?'

'Well, yes, but——'

'Don't apologise.' He kissed her gently. 'I like being seduced. I like playing games, and I don't mind people playing them with me, so long as they're nice games. Which this is.' He kissed her again, more lingeringly. 'But since I'm here, and you know I'm long past running away, you don't have to be so earnest about it. I like it when you flirt.' He pushed her down on to a sofa draped with fabric samples. 'Go on, drive me wild.'

'Not here!'

'Why not? The curtains are drawn. The door's locked,' he added, crossing to it and turning the key, which he threw across the room to her. 'Now you know you've got me trapped. So. Seduce me.'

'Why don't *you* seduce *me*?'

'Ah, but would you run?' He gave her a moment, then answered for her, 'No. But I will. So catch me.'

He wasn't running yet. He was standing by the door, legs apart, thumbs in his trouser pockets, taunting her with the wicked look in his blue eyes. She lay for a minute on the sofa where he'd tossed her, weighing his challenge.

Then she bent down and retrieved the key from the carpet. She slid it into the pocket of her brown corduroy skirt. She watched him watching her, letting her eyes feast on him. He was halfway across the room, but his look alone was enough to make her feel intensely aware of her own body, as well as of his.

Sexy, that was how she felt. She hadn't felt like this since she was a teenager. Grown-ups didn't do this. They didn't seduce each other in hotel conference-rooms. They didn't feel the sort of unruly passion that had them sick with impatience to get to bed.

Well. . .if they were Sean, they did. While if they were her. . .

She sat up. Slowly, her movements deliberately sensual, she slid her yellow sweater over her head. Her eyes back on him, she smoothed down her mussed-up hair. She unbuttoned her blouse.

She should have been wearing silk and lace underneath, wickedly seductive undies, instead of chain-store cotton. She'd never bought undies like that, never even worn the ones Neil had once or twice given her. She would go out the first free moment she got on Saturday and sweep up a shopful in Shanklin, she resolved.

But chain-store cotton felt seductive enough, when her breasts were swelling in anticipation, the nipples standing out proudly beneath the thin fabric. She let her blouse hang loose, shadowing them, as she slipped off her shoes.

Sean leaned against the door. She could feel the tension in him; feel skeins of desire tangling the room.

She nudged up her skirt, her gesture casual but deliberate, and watched him watching her as she peeled off her tights: first one leg, then the other. Then she stood up, unfastened her skirt, and let it fall to the floor at her feet.

A step, a slow step, towards him. And another. Then he ran.

He ducked past her, his speed taking her by surprise, vaulted the quilting frame, and came to a halt, half crouching, by the display of quilts at the end of the room.

Which way? Left? Right? She spun back to the sofa and pushed the end of it. It swung around easily on casters, blocking half the width of the room. Only one way now. She took it, feinting sideways as she approached him.

Sean caught a quilt from the top of the display. Ignoring the muffled thud of another two or three tumbling, he swirled it in front of him like a matador's cape.

Emma feinted again, rushed him, found herself caught in a swirl of heavy padded cotton. Sean spun her in it, laughing silently, cocooning her. Then ran again, lightly, quickly, pausing by the sofa.

'Damn you!' It took her several impatient seconds to shake herself free. She rushed him again. Sean leapt over the back of the sofa and backed to the door, brandishing something in his hand.

Her skirt. Oh, no, the key was in the pocket. He wouldn't. . .

Then let him. Don't rush: play. She paused, half crouching, her hands on the arm of the sofa; then took a deep breath, straightened up, and airily turned tail.

Back to the ruins of the quilt display, her back to him, shrugging off her blouse as she went. Without turning, she bent to flick the corner of a quilt from the floor. An easy twist of her body brought her behind it as she pulled it up, her hand held high, making it a curtain between them.

No—too clumsy. Casually, not glancing at him, she draped one end of the quilt over the book table, anchoring it with a pile of pattern books. Then, holding the other, she slipped back behind it, and gave Sean the quickest of glances as she reached her free hand to the catch of her bra.

He hadn't moved. She slid her bra off, catching it in her free hand and tossing it over the quilt barrier that hid her from his view. Turning her back to him, she let the hand that held the quilt just dip, as if by accident, before rapidly pulling it up again.

To slide off her panties one-handed while holding up a heavy quilt, keeping her movements graceful, was quite a feat. She managed it fairly well, she thought, and tossed them too over the quilt.

'What now?'

Sean's voice was light, but there was an edge of unsteadiness to it.

Good question. If she'd stopped to think, she might have felt a little idiotic now. He hadn't come a step closer, and he was still fully dressed. Her nakedness gave her an odd feeling of power, though, and there wasn't a tremor in her voice as she replied, quite airily, 'Perhaps I'll get dressed again.'

Without a moment's pause she dropped the quilt and stepped over it to retrieve her undies.

Before her hand touched them Sean was there. Catching her, pulling her hard against him.

'You call this running?' she teased, when she surfaced from the bruising power of his kiss.

'I call this driving me wild,' he murmured huskily. He picked her up bodily, and carried her over to the sofa. He lowered her on to it, then let his hands run down her, tracing the contours of her naked body.

Her response was immediate and intense. But she didn't flinch from it: she gloried in it, arching her body so that breasts and hips rose to greet his questing hands.

It was an agony, if a sweet one, when he drew away from her—although it was only to throw off his clothes. She watched him hungrily as navy pullover, grey shirt, grey trousers, socks and underpants joined the devastation around them.

Then he joined her on the sofa, and his running stopped for good.

CHAPTER NINE

'I SUPPOSE,' Emma murmured, 'I ought to get up.'

'Not yet.'

'Darling, it's a quarter to ten. I've barely time to dress before this morning's session.'

'Damn the session.' But there wasn't any conviction behind Sean's words, and he moved away the arm that had been holding her down against him.

She didn't get out of bed just yet, though, instead propping herself on one hand and leaning over him, smiling down at his tousled nakedness.

Sunday morning. It had been a glorious night, their second glorious night, and the second in which she'd barely slept. She didn't feel tired, though, so much as warmly exhilarated by their lovemaking.

'Want a shower?' she suggested.

'That'll leave you with no time for one.'

'We could shower together.'

'In ten minutes?'

'Mmm. I wish you were wrong, but I know you're not.'

'Spare me a kiss and I'll kick you out of bed.'

'I'm not sure I have any left.'

'Let's find out.'

Yes—yes, she could happily spend all morning doing more of what they'd been doing all night. But common sense and the quilt class called, and when Sean's hands and mouth released her she threw back the covers and started hunting for some clean clothes.

'What will you do this morning?' she asked, glancing

over at where Sean lay, hands behind his head, watching her move around, naked, as she assembled her outfit.

'Swim. Go for a walk. Phone my mother.'

'Phone your mother? Why?'

'I always do, Sunday mornings.'

'Oh.' Emma added a Fair Isle sweater to her pile. 'You never mention your mother.'

'I only think about her Sunday mornings. No, that's not fair,' he added, swinging his legs out of bed and following her to the bathroom. 'Or at least, only half fair. We have an arrangement. I always phone her Sunday at eleven, and she never bothers me the rest of the time.'

'Would she bother you if you didn't phone?'

'Are you kidding? It's taken me sixteen years to train her to keep out of my life.'

'And that's what you want from her?'

'What's this, an inquisition?'

'Sean, I don't ask you much,' Emma protested.

'Under the shower, woman.'

'It's important! I need to know. I need to understand you.'

'You're running out of time.'

'No, you are, Davies.' But she clambered into the bath and turned on the shower, conscious as she soaped herself of his tall figure on the other side of the semi-transparent curtain, and of the faint noises of him washing and shaving.

She drew the curtain back while she was drying herself, though she stayed in the bath so as not to crowd the smallish bathroom. And watched him, clad only in underpants, also getting ready to face the day.

Even now he was self-contained, she thought to herself. Over the previous thirty-six hours she had explored every inch of his firmly muscled body, but his mind was far less open to her. As a lover he was considerate, imaginative, energetic: all good things, all thoroughly desirable, but all, in a way, part of his social façade. He was still wary of letting her see the man behind the charming smile.

She wanted the rest. She wanted to know him inside out. She wanted to possess him.

But Sean didn't like the idea of being possessed.

And though becoming her lover had been a major step for him, one that he certainly hadn't taken lightly, it was still some way from being a total commitment. He hadn't poured out his heart to her; he hadn't made her any promises. Her patchwork-piece of his life had grown, but he hadn't placed it in the centre, and let the rest take shape around it. With every question she asked, she feared that he'd begin to feel trapped, and bolt for the door while it was still open to him.

Even so, it seemed to her that she didn't really have any option but to keep on pushing in the right direction. She needed more than this from him, and she wouldn't gain more by sitting back and waiting for him to open up to her. Pushing hard wouldn't be wise, but she did need to push.

How to catch a pike: slowly, slowly, with no reflections on the water.

'Do your parents live near you?' she asked casually, as she wandered, towel-clad, back through to the bedroom.

Sean sighed. 'In Enfield, maybe ten miles away. My sister's up the road from them. My dad's an accountant and my mum works in the local post office. Will that do you?'

'For now,' she agreed.

'*For now*?' he repeated, his voice almost threatening.

'Time's up, as you said.' She quickly slipped on the clothes from her pile, combed her hair, added lipstick and eyegloss, took a last gulp of cooling coffee from their breakfast tray. 'I'll see you for lunch, OK?'

'Em, we need to talk.'

'Later,' she assured him.

Their parting exchange didn't trouble her as she went down to the conference-room for the last-but-one session of the course, and soon the morning's frantic activity drove it from her mind. Sean hadn't forgotten it, however, and although there was no opportunity for them to talk over lunch he resumed the conversation that afternoon, as they were driving back to Newport.

'Em,' he said, 'I know it's been a great weekend, in every way. And I don't want to sour the end of it, but we've got to get this straight. I did mean it when I said I wasn't a marrying man.'

Emma's blood chilled—only momentarily, though, before she reminded herself that she had always expected a few setbacks along the way.

'Was I asking you to marry me?'

'Not in so many words, but that's the impression you put across.'

'Don't you think that's a bit—er—paranoid of you?'

'No.'

She took her eyes off the road to glance quickly at him, to find him looking straight back at her.

'I'm not a child or an idiot,' he said quietly. 'I've had relationships before, and I can read all the signs. I don't blame you, either. It's natural in your position to want commitment; it's what you need, and what Duncan needs too. But it's not what *I* need, Em, or what I want.'

'I'm not asking you to sacrifice yourself for us,' Emma said.

'Aren't you?'

Silence; a long silence.

'No,' she said awkwardly. 'Because it wouldn't work.

All right, I need more from you, but I don't want to take charity, Sean. I want a relationship from which we both gain.'

'So do I. And that's what we have now, so don't wreck it by asking for things I can't give.'

'But we could have more, so much more. We could share more; share our lives. All right—don't say it. You see that as my crowding you, trying to take you over, but I don't believe it would have to be like that. We could make a commitment and still leave each other space.'

'What space?'

'Well——'

He interrupted before she could frame her reply. 'I don't mean physical space, Em. I don't mean London, and I don't mean affairs with other women. What I need is space inside my head.'

'Not asking you questions.'

'Yes. No. I know it seems petty to you. You think, what's wrong with asking about my mum and dad?— and the answer is, there's nothing wrong. There's no ghastly secret to turn up; they're no different from other people's parents. But it's not just one question, love: it's the whole business of wanting to know somebody inside and out. I've seen it happen so often, and it destroys people.'

'People aren't that easily destroyed.'

'Aren't they?'

There was silence for a moment, then he went on, more vehemently, 'You don't know what it was like. When I was a kid my mum wanted to know everything. Where I'd been, where I was going, what I was thinking. She'd question my friends, she'd come into my bedroom, she'd have read my diary if I'd dared to write one.'

'I'm not like that,' Emma protested—but Sean wasn't listening.

'And it wasn't just me,' he continued. 'It was worse for my dad. All the time she'd nag away at him. She wanted to know where he was every minute. He couldn't watch a football match or buy a packet of cigarettes without her knowing about it. And do you know what happened? He'd cheat her. It got to be a thing with him to con her. He'd get friends to cover for him, he'd say he was at work when he wasn't, he even used to fiddle his wage packet so she didn't know how much was in it.'

'That's awful.'

'It was. Awful. It was a battle between them all the time. For years he'd do little things to spite her, like blowing a tenner he couldn't afford on a big race, or not coming home when she'd fixed to go out somewhere. Then it got so he had a whole secret life she didn't know about. There were always women, but then there was a serious woman, and then when I was twelve he left her. After that she turned it all on me, and I used to lie and cheat just like my Dad, so I could enjoy a drink or see a girl without her sticking her nose down my neck. Lord, I hated it! I swore I'd get away as soon as I could, and that was what I did. And I swore I'd never get married myself. I wasn't having anyone else pile all that on me.'

'Oh, Sean.'

'You can say it would be different with us,' he persisted, 'but it wouldn't be. All couples do it. Not as badly, maybe, but they all do. The world's full of paranoid insecure people who daren't leave their partners space for fear of what they'll do with it.'

'But Sean——'

'You've had a bad marriage,' he interrupted. 'You know what goes wrong. People expecting too much, people letting each other down. It doesn't work, Em.

I've had it up to here with lies and cheating, and now I don't promise what I can't give.'

Emma's hands were white on the steering-wheel. Her eyes had blurred, and she bit her lip as she tried to focus on the road.

It was horrible what he was saying, just horrible, and yet she could see an awful truth in it. It wasn't simply that he was sincere: he really had hit on a problem in close relationships. But to turn his back on them, because of that. . .!

'Mind,' Sean said harshly. His hand shot out and wrenched the steering-wheel, correcting her drift as a lorry bore down on them. 'Dammit, you're crying.'

'I'm not!'

'Stop the car, for heaven's sake.'

'There's nowhere to stop.'

'This'll do.' He nudged the wheel again, persuading her to turn on to a small side-road, and she slowly brought the car to a halt.

'Em, I'm sorry,' he said. 'I know I'm being mean, but you've got to understand. It's no good kidding yourself that you can go on getting more and more and more of me. I do love you, but I want to stay my own man too. I want to keep my own space, and that's not going to change.'

She turned her back on him. It was ridiculous to be crying. She didn't want him to see it. He might think she was doing it to manipulate him, but that wasn't it; she was only crying because she couldn't stop.

'You've got to ride with it, love,' Sean said, more gently. 'Not push, just let things happen. Who was it said—it's not the arrival, it's the journey that matters? We're happy now. We've been happy all this weekend, amazingly happy. I want us to stay like this. I don't want us to wreck it by asking for too much.'

'But. . .' She took a heaving breath, and tried again. 'It's not enough, Sean. All right, we've been happy, but one of the reasons I've been happy is because I thought our relationship was growing. It has been growing. It's not just me; we've both been learning about each other, giving more and more to each other. I want that to carry on. I don't want to push you, or pry into things you want to keep private, but I want it to keep on growing. All right, it might not lead to marriage, but——'

'It won't,' Sean interrupted.

'But it's going to keep on growing,' she persisted. 'I can't just let it rest like this—it's not enough. I don't want to crowd you, but I do *need* more than this. I need to understand you better, so I can feel close to you. I need to know you so I can trust you. That's what you don't talk about: trust. Trust isn't imaginary. It isn't easy to bring about, but it grows with commitment and security and love. That's what I want, the kind of trust that enables people to share their lives. Not taking everything, not stealing all their partner's space, but being a partnership, in a way we're not, yet.'

'Em, you've got to stop pushing.'

'Then you've got to start giving, for heaven's sake!' She turned brimming eyes on him. 'I wouldn't need to push, Sean, if you were letting it ride, but *you're not*. You've got the brakes full on, and you have had all along.'

'You don't understand,' Sean said tautly.

'No, I don't. You're scared, and of what? Of my insecurity? But you make me insecure, by not giving me the commitment I need!'

'You can't have commitments. Commitments lead to lies—that's what I'm trying to tell you.'

'They don't have to.'

'Yes, they do.' He unfastened his seatbelt. Emma's eyes widened. Oh, no! He wouldn't——

Sean got out of the car, strode round the bonnet, and opened the driver's door. 'Shift over,' he said. 'I'll drive us home.'

'No. I don't want to——'

'No arguments. We're getting nowhere, we're just fouling things up. Maybe I shouldn't have said all that now, but hell, it needed saying. We're not going to carry on like this, though, getting you in a state. We'll go right back, then I'll go off to London for a while and give you a chance to think it over.'

'*Me* to think it over!'

'Yes, you. Because I'm not going to change, Em. So you've got to decide whether you want us to carry on as we are.'

By the time they reached Newport Emma had recovered her surface calm, repaired her make-up, and was just about ready to face her parents and Duncan. Inside, though, she felt numb and wretched.

It was still hard to believe that he meant it. After a weekend in which everything had gone their way, he'd not only taken two steps back: he'd announced that he would never move forward any further.

He did mean it, though. He wasn't a cruel man, and she knew he wouldn't have forced the scene they had just been through if he hadn't honestly believed it was necessary.

And if he was right, if he wasn't going to come round to her way of thinking, then she really did need the break he was suggesting, while she reconsidered the situation.

Judy's metaphor had taken her only so far. She had been planning how to catch her pike, and all right, she'd hooked him. But she hadn't thought through to what the pike would feel like, gasping on the riverbank. Perhaps it was hardly surprising that this pike couldn't wait to jump back into the water.

Charming as ever, Sean paused to hear about Duncan's weekend, to chat briefly to her parents, and to provide a little cover when her misery temporarily threatened to overwhelm her. He retreated next door, then called round again half an hour later with the news—concocted largely for Duncan's sake—that urgent work was calling him back to London.

'When are you coming back?' Duncan demanded. 'I've hardly seen you, Sean. You haven't played my new computer game or *anything*.'

'Soon,' Sean assured him. 'I'll phone you, Em. OK?'

'OK,' she managed to reply. And she kept her composure, just, as he crossed to kiss her forehead and squeeze her arm. It was only when he whispered, 'I do love you', that the tears prickled; and, seeing them, he hastily completed his goodbyes to the rest of her family, and set off for the ferry.

For once, it was a blessing that her parents weren't observant enough, or interested enough in her life, to notice her low mood or ask her much about Sean. Her mother did comment on how fond Duncan seemed of him, and ask whether there was any prospect of marriage—but Emma could honestly reply 'no' to that, and that ended the conversation.

It was also a blessing that her parents were still around when Rose Frazer appeared to collect her next batch of quilts. Emma needed some moral support in negotiating, and her bluff, no-nonsense father was just the person to provide it.

She had drawn up a written agreement, slightly adapted from the one Celia had provided, and with the new quilts to use as bargaining counters, and her father's silent determination backing her up, she didn't find it too difficult to persuade Mrs Frazer to sign it.

'Only three, though?' Mrs Frazer protested. 'I thought you were going to let us have more than that!'

She really hadn't *got* any more, Emma thought ruefully. At the quilting weekend she had sold both of the quilts she'd taken for sale, plus one of her competition winners for which she'd received an irresistible offer, and that had taken her already depleted stock down to drought level. She had had to talk Sean out of his half-formed idea of giving a quilt to Lillie for Christmas, and heaven knew when she'd be able to offer more to Celia. From the desperation of that September, things had improved so fast that now she simply couldn't match the demand for her work!

'The only one I've left to offer is a very special hand-sewn one,' she explained. 'I'd really rather not sell it, since I won my first-ever big competition with it, and to be frank I don't think it would be suitable for Favourite Things. I'd have to ask at least five hundred pounds for it, and——'

'Five hundred! That's ridiculous!'

'Not when you allow for the work that's gone into it,' Emma contended. 'Compare it to a painting or sculpture, and it's really remarkably cheap.'

'You might think so, but I couldn't sell anything at that price.'

'Then three will have to do till I've had time to make some more. I'm working flat out, Mrs Frazer, and I'll have another couple finished very soon.'

'Bring them over as soon as you've finished them,' Mrs Frazer insisted, and Emma assured her that she would do just that.

It was only after Mrs Frazer and her van had disappeared that Emma's mother suggested she might have asked for payment for the quilts that had been sold.

Emma was dubious. 'I did get the written agreement,' she pointed out, 'and it would have been stretching the Frazers' tolerance to ask for anything else. We agreed on payment at the end of each month, and the shop hasn't been open a fortnight yet.'

'Isn't it normal to make December payments before Christmas, though?'

'Not that normal, although it's true that it is sometimes done—and I have been paying out a lot for more fabric and wadding. Perhaps I'll raise the subject when I take the next couple of quilts over.'

After her parents' departure she threw herself into work, and the quilts began to take shape fast. It was good therapy, keeping her from thinking too much about Sean.

After all, what was there to think over? He'd left her with a dilemma, and she didn't know how to resolve it, but it wasn't a question of understanding it better: she understood the situation only too clearly. She couldn't imagine giving him up, but she knew she wouldn't be happy with a long-term relationship lived on his terms.

'Let things drift for a while,' was Judy's advice. 'Your relationship has developed so fast! Give Sean time to come to terms with it. You can afford the time; after all, you're not going anywhere else, are you?'

No, she wasn't. After what she and Sean had shared, she had lost even the faint interest she had once worked up in marrying for the sake of security. Half a relationship with Sean would be far better than that! But when she looked ahead and imagined weeks and years drifting by, a long expanse in which her and Duncan's hunger for love and security was fuelled by Sean's evasiveness and unwillingness to commit himself, then the prospect horrified her.

If he had left any room for doubt; if he had let things drift himself, then she might have seen the situation differently. He had been so clear, though; so adamant. There wasn't any hope that he might change his mind. And wasn't it the case that the longer she let their affair continue, the harder she would find it to end it eventually?

Sean had phoned two days after he had left, and she'd asked him to give her more time. They had chatted for a while, but he hadn't pressed her. He phoned again, two days after that—and she told him not to phone again.

'Em, are you sure?' he said urgently.

'As sure as I can be.'

'This isn't what I meant to happen. I don't want us to break up, darling.'

'Then say you'll work on it,' Emma pleaded. 'Say you'll make a real effort to open up to me. It can be as slowly as you like, but say you'll give our relationship a chance to develop.'

'Em, you're asking for what I can't give.'

'Then you're asking for what I can't give, too,' she replied, and put the phone down on him.

Afterwards she cried. Not nicely, but in a loud, ugly, hopeless way. Then the time came for Duncan to come home from school, so she splashed her face with cold water and tried to get on with life without Sean.

It wasn't easy. She had lost the fervour with which she had thrown herself into work. Days seemed to go by, and at the end of each one she would need to splash her face with cold water—and at the end of each one she would realise to her horror that she had sewn only a handful of seams, quilted only a few square inches.

It was almost a fortnight before she had two quilts

ready to take over to Ryde. Christmas was only a few days off—and a lousy Christmas it was likely to be, she thought gloomily. She had sounded out Judy and some of her other friends to see if she and Duncan might share their celebrations, but they had all been disappointingly non-committal, so it looked as if the two of them would be alone.

At least she had no money worries. Mrs Frazer's original sales had been no fluke, it seemed: every few days she had been calling to announce the sale of another quilt. When she was paid for them, Emma would be able to afford to pay off a large chunk of her overdraft, and still buy Duncan the racing bike he had set his heart on.

A bike wasn't much of a substitute for Sean. Duncan was missing Sean, and he didn't miss any opportunity to tell Emma so. She hated herself for having caused him this unhappiness. She still believed she had made the right decision, but Duncan couldn't be expected to understand why.

Still, the bike would do something to lift his spirits, and it was good that she could afford it—or almost afford it. She had paid the shop a deposit already, but she really needed Mrs Frazer's cheque right away, so that she could pay the balance too before Christmas.

So? With the new quilts to deliver, it surely wouldn't be too unreasonable for her to push for it.

A bell tinkled as she pushed open the big glass door of the gift shop. She paused, glancing round. Only three quilts were hanging on the walls, where there had been six for the launch. Had still more been sold?

'Oh, hi, Emma.'

'Hello, Mrs Jackson.' Emma urged some brightness into her voice, recognising the old acquaintance who had commissioned a Log Cabin quilt from her, back in the autumn. 'I didn't expect to see you here.'

'Actually it was a shock to me too, to see your work here. I mean, it's nice to be able to afford a quilt for Lindsay's bedroom, but when I see the prices here it's hard not to feel a bit put out, you know.'

'How do you mean?' Emma asked, taking in the fact that Mrs Frazer was busily wrapping up a large bundle—the quilt Mrs Jackson was buying for Lindsay, presumably.

'Well! When I think what we paid for the Log Cabin! I thought we'd got a good deal commissioning one directly from you, but it's obvious now that you charged us through the nose. We haven't money to burn, you know. And to think my neighbour bought a quilt just as nice as ours for less than half the price we paid. . .'

'That can't be so.' Emma shook her head, bewildered. 'Unless it was a single-bed size, maybe—or a factory-made one.'

'No, it was one of yours, from here.'

'All done, Mrs Jackson,' Rose Frazer announced, tying the last knot in her string.

'But I don't understand. I wouldn't cheat you, Mrs Jackson. Almost all the quilts I've been selling here cost more than I charged you for the Log Cabin. I don't know which one you've picked for Lindsay, but——'

'Could I have a word with you, Mrs Morgan?' Mrs Frazer cut in.

'Just a minute. I've got to know what's going on here. Which one have you bought?'

'It's a pink and green one, with roses.'

'The Double Wedding-Ring? But that's one of my hand-sewn quilts! With the VAT, that must have cost you almost twice as much as——'

'Mrs Morgan!'

'Ninety-nine pounds,' Mrs Jackson announced, picking up her parcel.

'Ninety-nine pounds! But——'

'So now you know why I'm livid.'

Mrs Jackson headed for the door, and Emma collecting her thoughts, turned to rush after her.

'Mrs Morgan!'

'Let go!' she spat, trying to shake Rose Frazer's hand off her sleeve as Mrs Jackson disappeared down the street.

'I will not! What do you think you're doing, trying to upset my customers?'

'What am *I* doing? What are *you* doing? Ninety-nine pounds? Is that some kind of joke? Because it's a pretty sick joke, I can tell you!'

'Now calm down! It's a very reasonable price.'

'Reasonable! That's barely as much as the materials cost! For a hand-sewn quilt! There's over a hundred hours of labour in that quilt!'

'Don't be ridiculous,' Mrs Frazer said sharply. 'You can't expect anyone to pay more than a hundred pounds for a patchwork quilt.'

'You can't——' She stopped dead, suddenly struck by the awful reality of the situation. 'Oh, my God.'

'Realism's the first rule in this trade,' Mrs Frazer was saying, in a briskly defensive voice. 'You wouldn't believe the amounts some people expect their work to fetch, but when you're running a chain of shops you soon learn how to price things realistically. Turnover's the name of our game. All that stuff you had mouldering away in your upstairs room, and we've turned it into hard cash for you. Ten quilts sold in less than a month. That's efficiency for you, my dear.'

'Oh, my God,' Emma repeated. Her legs felt about to give way, and she had to lean on the shop counter. 'You've—sold—them—all. For ninety-nine pounds.'

'A great success they've been, too.'

'But I priced them. I did the swing-tags. You must have seen——'

'You couldn't have expected us to ask *those* prices, dear,' Mrs Frazer said. She had switched now to a sickeningly conciliatory tone. 'Anyway, you came to the launch. You saw we'd repriced them.'

'I what?'

'There's a label on every one, just the same as on all our stock.'

In a daze, Emma crossed the shop. She paused just below the point where her sunburst quilt hung on the wall. At least that hadn't sold. It had been Sean's favourite. Ninety-nine pounds. The label was there; a tiny label with a printed price, right in the corner, high up so that she had to crane to read it.

She hadn't craned to read the labels at the launch, not with the room crowded. Nor had Judy. She hadn't even put a price clause in the written contract.

'Have you got a stepladder?'

'Mrs Morgan! What are you doing?'

Finding the long ladder in the far corner of the shop, that was what. Propping it up, climbing it, reaching up to unpin the quilt from where it had been fastened to a batten on the wall.

'We've a contract, don't forget,' Mrs Frazer was saying, buzzing around down below her. 'A written contract, just as you asked for. You can't just take them away, my girl, not when you've signed a contract.'

'Damn the contract,' said Emma, and kept on unpinning the quilt.

CHAPTER TEN

TELLING Duncan he couldn't have his racing bike for Christmas was one of the hardest things Emma had ever done. If there had been any alternative she wouldn't have done it—but there wasn't.

Ten quilts lost. Sold for a fraction of their worth, by a woman who was now complaining that Emma had broken her own contract in claiming back the few unsold ones, and threatening not to pay up even the small sum that was due. Her lynchpin contract in ruins, no stock left, her link with Celia's craft shop and the Prince Regent destroyed. She hadn't any money in hand, and she couldn't see how she could possibly recover the situation.

'As soon as I can possibly afford it, I'll get you the bike,' she assured Duncan. 'The shopkeeper's promised to hold it till Easter, and I'll do everything I can, love. But you have to understand, I can't promise anything. At the best of times I can only just hold my head above water, and with all my stock gone, and a slack season coming up, I can't expect good times to be round the corner.'

'Can't Sean help?' Duncan asked.

'No,' Emma said heavily.

She spent a couple of miserable days sorting through her fabric stocks, trying to work out how many quilts she could assemble without buying more fabric, which she simply couldn't afford. Then Judy came round, and she gave in to her despair and had a good howl to her friend.

Judy, bless her, made coffee and listened and dispensed sympathy and understanding.

'And at Christmas,' Emma wailed. 'It's only a couple of days off, and I've been so worried about the work that I haven't even started to get things ready. I know there's only Duncan and me, but it wouldn't be fair to Duncan to skimp too much on it. There's no way I can buy the bike, but I'll get him as many of the smaller things he wants as I can, and I need to put up some decorations, and then there's the food. I've barely thought about the food yet. Maybe not a turkey, but. . .'

'It's as well you haven't thought about it,' Judy assured her.

'And what's that supposed to mean? Honestly, Judy!'

'Sorry, I shouldn't have said that. Look, Em, leave the work for now. I've just got to make a phone call, then you come out with me and we'll do your Christmas shopping. School holidays tomorrow, so you ought to get Duncan's presents today. We'll have a good scour around and see what we can find him, OK?'

'OK,' Emma listlessly agreed. She assembled a rapid list while Judy made her call—to Tom, presumably—and then they set out for the shops together.

Judy's determined cheerfulness soon had its effect, and Emma's spirits brightened a little. She picked out an imitation Portsmouth football strip that she knew Duncan would love, and a couple of new computer games for him, as well as small presents for other relations and friends she hadn't yet bought for. Judy was warmly complimentary on her skill in choosing the right presents—typically Taurean, she teased—although Emma bridled when her friend advised her to pick out something for Sean.

'I won't be seeing Sean,' she protested.

'Obviously you will,' Judy said bluntly. 'He's your

next-door neighbour, Em—he can't just disappear from Newport. And even if you two have had a tiff Tom and I are still friends with him, and so are Marie and Ted—and I bet Duncan isn't going to give up going round to see him!'

'It wasn't a tiff, Jude. And don't start telling me I was wrong to end it, because I couldn't stand that at the moment.'

'No, you weren't wrong,' Judy gently assured her. 'You need some security, and you were right to hold out for it. But what you two really need is to split your differences, not to break up over them. After all, Sean might grumble at feeling tied down, but you weren't really looking for so much more than you already had from him, were you?'

'On a day-to-day basis, I suppose not,' Emma agreed. 'It was the feeling of security I needed; knowing he'd always be around. Being a partnership, so that when something like this mess with the Frazers happened, I'd have someone to turn to—and doing the same for him, of course, when he needed support. But that's what Sean wouldn't give me.'

'Maybe you pushed too hard.'

'Maybe I did. Anyway, it's too late now.'

'It isn't too late until you're dead,' Judy retorted. 'So be a good girl and pick out some records he'd like. If you're too hard up, *I'll* pay for them.'

'A tenner won't break me,' Emma conceded, and spent a bitter-sweet few minutes deciding which of the new releases would most appeal to Sean.

By then it was time for the children to come out of school, and it didn't take much persuading for her to bring Duncan back to Judy's house for tea.

She was sitting on the sofa in Judy's front room with

Duncan, looking over the drawings that he had brought home from school, when the doorbell rang.

'Em, can you answer it?' Judy called. 'I'm tied up in the kitchen.'

'Tom's back early,' Emma commented.

But it wasn't Tom. It was Sean.

She would have slammed the door as soon as she saw him, if his foot hadn't beaten her to it. Since it had, though, her only escape route was to the kitchen.

'Judy, how could you?'

'He was coming tomorrow anyway,' Judy responded, half her mind on the mince pies she was taking out of the oven. 'I just speeded it up—hi, Sean—by telling him about the Frazers. Although it was a pretty daft plan, Sean: you might have guessed Em would spend days getting ready for Christmas down here.'

'I have,' Emma retorted, edging away from Sean's tall figure. 'And I don't want you to——'

'You're outvoted,' Sean said calmly. 'Two to one. Isn't that right, Dunc? Christmas in London; it's time you came up to my place. Anyway, I haven't brought your racing bike down with me, Duncan, so if you want to get it on Christmas Day you'll have to stick up for my plan.'

'My racing bike! Hey, that's great!'

'So much for surprises,' Judy said dourly.

'I can't afford not to play my trumps,' Sean pointed out. 'I haven't won yet. Judy, be a love and keep an eye on this lad for five minutes while I talk to his mum.'

'You're not going *already*,' Duncan protested.

'Only in the living-room. Come on, Em.'

'I haven't got anything to say to you.'

'So I'll do the talking,' Sean retorted. He uncurled his red scarf from round his neck, lassoed Emma with it, and began to haul her towards the door.

'Judy——'

'This time,' Judy assured her, 'you're very definitely outvoted.'

Confusedly, barely able to be angry and yet not daring to hope, Emma followed Sean into Judy's living-room. He shut the door behind them, then turned back to her and took her in his arms.

'Sean, please,' she said tremblingly.

'Shut up, woman.'

She hadn't much choice, since he was kissing her in a way that didn't leave any room at all for conversation. And in spite of her resolutions the touch and taste of him was working all its usual magic on her.

'Love me?' he asked quietly, when the first fervour of their kisses had given way to a calmer embrace.

'You know I do.'

'I love you too. Didn't mean to, but I do. And it's been hell without you these past couple of weeks.'

'I know, but Sean——'

'Shush.' He kissed her again. 'How am I supposed to give in gracefully when you keep on interrupting me?'

'To *what*?'

'Well, fairly gracefully. Want your Christmas present now?'

'It depends on what it is.'

'Your detective work's lacking, my dear.' He released her, though only to fumble in the pockets of his jacket. 'At least,' he continued, holding out a small square box, 'I thought that was what you wanted? Roughly? I mean if you don't like the ring we can always swap it, but——'

'Sean!'

Like it? It was beautiful! Classic diamonds in a heavy gold setting, just the engagement ring every woman dreamed of.

'You do like it,' Sean said complacently.

'Of course I do.' It was her turn to kiss him now, as soon as she had helped him slip it on her finger. 'But Sean, when did you——?'

'Don't know, really—in slow stages, I suppose,' he said consideringly, sweeping Duncan's drawings off the sofa and pulling her down to join him in the space he'd cleared. 'I'd fixed on bringing you up to London for Christmas as soon as I knew you and Duncan were going to be on your own. Then when you told me you wanted to break things off, I thought about scrapping the idea, but I couldn't imagine a Christmas without you. I'd got really keen on the idea of having the two of you around, taking you places, showing you things, having you meet my friends. So then I thought, how can I make her come? And this was the obvious way.'

'But you were so determined not to get married.'

'So I was,' he agreed. 'At first I thought, no, I can't. Walking into the cage and closing the door behind me; it's just not my thing. But when I really thought about it I couldn't see what I was scared of. You're not the pushy type, and you've never tried to take over my life. You know I need space, and you've always let me have it. Anyway, it's got to the stage where the space is starting to look empty when you and Duncan aren't around to fill it. So I'd come around far enough to buy the ring, although I still wasn't absolutely certain, when Judy rang this afternoon. And then it angered me so much, knowing that I hadn't been there when you needed me, and *wanting* to be there, that I knew I'd been right—and that I had to get down here straight away.'

'Which you did,' Emma said wonderingly.

'Three hours door to door—not bad. Mind, I didn't need to pack, because I meant to take you straight back to London with me. You *will* come?'

'Of course we will,' Emma assured him.

'We'll have a great Christmas. I owe Judy a favour, though; she said she felt awful, stringing you along when you thought you'd nowhere to go, and she knew all the time what I was planning! I wanted to surprise you at the last moment, but I guess that wasn't one of my brighter schemes.'

'I like your crazy ideas. I've loved them from the moment you first jumped into my car.'

'Liar,' Sean said affectionately. 'You'll learn to love them, though. As Judy says, your Taurean nature needs a little stirring-up now and again!'

'And your Aquarian nature needs a little ballast! But you do know, Sean,' she went on, more seriously, 'that it's going to mean a lot of changes in your life?'

'True, and there's lots to sort out. Even where we'll live; maybe we'll stay here permanently, but maybe you'll like London more when you see my house and my friends up there. Getting to know you and Duncan really brought it home to me how much I was missing you both in my life.'

'Do you want more children?'

'Maybe: we'll talk it over with Duncan before we decide. But what I want right now is for all three of us to be happy.'

'I am,' Emma assured him, overjoyed that the Aquarius in him had given way to love. 'Incredibly happy.'

'And so am I,' Sean agreed. 'And so will Duncan be, I hope, as soon as we tell him—so let's go and do that now!'

STARGAZING

YOUR STAR SIGN: **TAURUS (April 21–May 21)**

TAURUS is the second sign of the Zodiac, ruled by the planet Venus and controlled by the element of Earth. These make you obstinate, purposeful, reliable and—sometimes—rather self-righteous. Your high degree of motivation, endurance and need for security makes you carry out plans thoroughly with resolute attention to details—up to the point of stubbornness!

Socially, Taureans are known for their motto: 'Eat, drink and be merry'—you possess an earthy sense of humour and have a pragmatic approach to life in general. As the second and most fertile sign in the Zodiac, building a secure and comfortable home is your main concern and every effort is directed towards that goal.

Your characteristics in love: Charming and dependable, Taureans tend to be incurable romantics and enjoy giving presents to their loved ones. They are loyal when it comes to relationships but like to take things at snail's pace to be extra sure of sweethearts before committing themselves. Nevertheless, once you are in love, you are an extremely faithful partner to the extent of being possessive and see red once the bull in you is unleashed. You prefer to choose marriage rather than living together with your ideal partner since it helps boost your craving for security.

Signs which are compatible with you: Capricorn, **Virgo**, **Cancer** and **Pisces** are the most harmonious, while **Gemini**, **Sagittarius** and **Aquarius** provide you with a challenge. Partners born under other signs can be compatible, depending on which planets reside in their Houses of Personality and Romance.

What is your star-career? Taurean philosophy is to take root and then grow when it comes to career matters. Once an appropriate career is found, such as music, industry, building, landscape gardening and accountancy, you will work with steadfast enthusiasm and develop skills without being confronted by any sudden changes.

Your colours and birthstones: Taureans have a good sense of colour and feel soothed by the colour of the sky: pale blue and pink but never red—as any bull fighter will tell you.

Your birthstones are diamonds and emeralds; both stones enhance the practical femininity of a Taurean as well as being a good investment. Diamonds are the purest tokens of love, while the emerald has a tradition of healing eye diseases. Even today, some believe that tired eyes can be revived with water in which an emerald has been soaked overnight.

TAURUS ASTRO-FACTFILE

Day of the week: Friday.
Countries: USSR, Ireland and Cyprus.
Flowers: Violet and poppy.
Food: Oysters and Dover sole; Taureans are great food-lovers and have acute tastebuds but—being creatures of habit—they will stick with their favourite recipes.
Health: Although you have a sturdy constitution, take care not to over-indulge in the good life—or you might regret it later on in life! Watch your weight and treat yourself to sensual therapies such as body massage and saunas.

You share your star sign with these famous names:

Perry Como
Michael Palin
Lloyd Honeyghan
Peter Howitt
Pope John Paul II

Cher
Queen Elizabeth II
Maureen Lipman
Audrey Hepburn
Selina Scott

ZODIAC LOVE MATCH

CALL THE MILLS & BOON
LOVE MATCH HOTLINE

The only service to give you a detailed love analysis of your own star sign and then tell you how romantically compatible you are with the man of your dreams.

If you're interested in hearing how you match up with that special man in your life, or just want to know who would suit you best, all you have to know is your own star sign and that of the man you're interested in hearing yourself matched with.

If you dial the special Love Match 'phone number shown below, we will connect you to Catriona Roberts Wright who will give you an in-depth report on how compatible your two signs are.

CAN YOU BEAR TO WAIT?

Mills & Boon

Next month's Romances

Each month, you can choose from a world of variety in romance with Mills & Boon. These are the new titles to look out for next month.

WHEN THE DEVIL DRIVES Sara Craven

PAYMENT DUE Penny Jordan

LAND OF DRAGONS Joanna Mansell

FLIGHT OF DISCOVERY Jessica Steele

LEAVE LOVE ALONE Lindsay Armstrong

THE DEVIL'S KISS Sally Wentworth

THE IRON MASTER Rachel Ford

BREAKING THE ICE Kay Gregory

STEPS TO HEAVEN Sally Heywood

A FIERY ENCOUNTER Margaret Mayo

A SPECIAL SORT OF MAN Natalie Fox

MASTER OF MARSHLANDS Miriam Macgregor

MISTAKEN LOVE Shirley Kemp

BROKEN DREAMS Jennifer Williams

STOLEN KISSES Debbie Macomber

STARSIGN

DOUBLE DECEIVER Rebecca King

Available from Boots, Martins, John Menzies, W.H. Smith, Woolworths and other paperback stockists.

Also available from Mills and Boon Reader Service, P.O. Box 236, Thornton Road, Croydon, Surrey CR9 3RU.